THE PHANTOM OF EERIE HOLLOW

The Phantom of Eerie Hollow

Book Cover Design by Neal Hopkin

www.truehunter.com

First Printing 2024

The Phantom of Eerie Hollow

CLINT ELLSWORTH

To every kid that loves a good hunting mystery.

You can find Crazy Carl's spooky song at:
www.TrueHunter.com

Contents

Chapter 1

Moving On

"And there I was, standing face to face with a psychotic grizzly bear. He stood every bit of ten feet tall. His dark fur was matted with blood from past victims. He swiped the air with his dagger-like claws. His eyes were an evil red. He thirsted for my blood, but I stood my ground. I looked that sucker in his demon-like eyes. I curled my upper lip. He growled a ferocious roar. Spit flew from his mouth and hit me in the face. I raised my dad's pistol into the air and took aim. Nobody spits in my face and gets away with it. Not even a crazy grizzly...."

"Sure, Jack. I totally believe you," I said with more than a hint of sarcasm in my voice.

I reached down and picked up a box from the moving truck. I made my way down the cobblestone driveway to my new home. My cousin Jack was quite the storyteller, that's for sure.

"McKay! Never interrupt a hunter when he is telling an honest-to-goodness hunting story. I'm not done yet. Where was I?" Jack said as he picked up a box of hunting stuff from the moving truck.

He ran to catch up to me. We walked side by side through the giant double oak doors of the old, spooky mansion I would now call home.

Jack continued with his ridiculous story, "I let out a fierce growl of my own as I cocked the .357 Magnum pistol. The psycho grizzly's bloodshot eyes dared me to pull the trigger. So, that's what I did. The blast threw me backward. It was like I was in slow motion. As I fell back, I watched as the bullet ripped through the flesh of the killer bear's face. His right ear flew off his head and landed five feet behind him on the tundra floor. I stood up and yelled at the injured bear," Jack shared as he cocked his head sideways.

He told the story like it was no big deal. He let out a cocky sigh.

"The psycho grizzly whipped his head side to side in pain from the bullet that had torn through his face. The gash on his cheek dripped blood down to his razor-like teeth. He must have realized I was the superior predator because he dropped onto all fours. He growled one last time, turned, and ran with his tiny tail tucked between his legs!" bragged Jack.

"I honestly don't believe a word you just said," I challenged, shaking my head in disbelief.

I turned away from Jack as I put the box on the marble floor in the mansion's entryway.

"Oh, if you don't believe me, let's give Sienna a call. She was right there with me the whole time. I'll call her right now," Jack responded as he strolled over to the fancy phone on the wall on the other side of the oversized foyer.

"Who is Sienna?" I asked.

I raised my eyebrows high with curiosity. I tried not to show any sort of interest, but I was intrigued, to say the least.

"Oh, Sienna is probably the most amazing girl on the planet. We met when I was eight, and she was fourteen. So, I guess that would make her eighteen now. You could say we're pretty close, kind of like flint and steel."

"Oh, I'm sure an eighteen-year-old girl is friends with a twelve-year-old boy," I smirked, calling out his obvious lie.

Jack dialed a number on the phone. He put the phone up to his ear. I put my head next to his so I could listen to see if the phone actually rang on the other end. I figured he would just dial a fake number and pretend to talk to a girl, but to my astonishment, the phone began to ring. You can only imagine how shocked I was to actually hear a girl's voice answer the phone.

"Hi! This is Sienna," replied the voice on the other end of the phone.

"Hey, Sienna, it's Jack."

"Jack! Long time no talk. How are you doing? Have you shot any psycho grizzlies in the face lately?" she joked.

Jack looked at me and nodded with a cocky smile. His light blue eyes danced with pride.

"That's why I'm calling. My cousin, McKay, says he doesn't believe a single word about how we scared off that crazy ol' Grizz. Could you back my story up? Here's McKay," Jack said.

He handed me the phone. I suddenly got nervous. It wasn't every day that I talked to a girl on the phone, and I had no clue what to say.

"Umm, hi, Sienna. This is McKay. I'm Jack's cousin. Umm... Did Jack really shoot a grizzly in the face?" I asked awkwardly.

"McKay, I know it's hard to believe. I wouldn't believe it either if I wasn't there, but he did. Jack saved my life!" she exclaimed.

"See, I told you!" Jack shouted loudly.

He flexed his muscles at me and nodded his head like he was some kind of hot shot.

"Oh, wow. OK. Thanks. Nice talking to you, Sienna," I stammered.

I handed the phone back to Jack, who told Sienna he'd call her again some other time. I shook my head from side to side in disbelief, looked at Jack, and sighed.

Jack and I had known each other our whole lives. My mom and his dad were siblings. His dad, my uncle Dallas, was a huge, very strong man. He looked like a real Viking Chief! He had a long, blonde, braided beard that ran down to his belt. His barrel chest was the size of a refrigerator, and his arms were as big as rolled-up sleeping bags. I was always surprised that he could find shirts that could fit over his massive biceps without ripping.

It was pretty odd because my mom and Dallas were not built the same way at all. She was short—I don't think she was even five feet tall. Her arms were slender but toned. Her hair was brown, not blonde like Dallas's. They didn't look like siblings in the slightest way.

Everyone always joked that Dallas got the muscles and my mom got the brains. My mom was sharp, no doubt about it. There was no fooling her about any-thing. She always knew when I was stretching the truth, and she wasn't somebody you wanted to cross. I made that mistake a few careless times in my life, and I'm lucky to have lived to tell the tale. But there was a softer side to her. She was kind and loving. I knew she wanted me to grow up to be the best version of myself.

Just then, Mom walked through the double oak doors into the spacious entryway with a moving box in her arms.

"What are you two troublemakers up to? Why aren't you unloading the moving truck?" she asked, with squinted eyes and a slightly tilted head.

"Sorry, Mom. Jack and I were just talking about how he shot a grizzly in the face. Have you ever heard that story?"

"Yes, yes, I have. Your uncle Dallas has shared that experience with your dad and me a few times over the years. I've heard that Jack is a lucky boy to have survived that day."

She paused momentarily and looked Jack in the eyes, "Are you still having nightmares about that scary grizzly bear?" Mom asked.

Jack's face turned red. I don't think I had ever seen Jack so embarrassed before. He broke eye contact with my mom and looked down at the ground.

"Nightmares? Nightmares? I don't know what you are talking about. I don't have nightmares. I'm not scared of anything...."

Just then, my dad stumbled into the room, taking all the attention from Jack's embarrassed denials. Dad and Dallas were carrying our large, heavy couch. My dad's face was red, and he was making a lot of grunting noises. His arms were shaking. I looked over at Dallas. He smiled and winked at me. He seemed to be handling his end of the couch effortlessly.

"McKay! Help!" Dad called out urgently.

I ran over and grabbed his side of the couch. As soon as I got a grip on it, my dad let go, and the full weight of his side of the couch transferred to my arms.

"Thank you, McKay! You're a lifesaver. Why don't you help your uncle put the couch in that big empty room over there?" Dad asked.

A little grin appeared on his face, knowing full well that he used his son to get out of carrying the oversized couch. While I struggled to move the couch, he sat on a chair by Jack to rest for a moment. Dad was a trickster. Mom was always blaming him for my "playful" behavior.

"I see what you did there, Dad. Don't worry. Your twelve-year-old son will do all the heavy lifting for you," I grunted.

"Oh, you won't be doing all the heavy lifting. That's why Jack and Dallas are here," he joked as he slapped Jack on the back.

Jack gave him a courtesy laugh. It was kind of funny, but it was true. Dallas and Jack brought their muscles all the way from Alaska to help my family move into this new home.

Well, it's not exactly "new." You know those old, giant mansions that are definitely haunted? Well... it's one of those....

Chapter 2

The Lawyer

A few months ago, there was a knock at our old house where we used to live. I ran down the stairs to answer it.

I figured it was just my buddy from down the street wanting to play ball. As I ran past it, I grabbed my baseball glove, which was lying on the bottom of the stairs. I quickly whipped the door open, thinking I would catch my friend off guard, but instead, I was the one who was startled.

Standing on my doorstep was a tall, gangly man dressed in a black suit. He had black-rimmed glasses and slicked-down black hair. His shoes were black. Everything was black except for a hideous, yellow tie that looked like a dog had barfed on it. The man's hands were full. In his right hand was a black briefcase that he held by its leather handle. He carefully held a fancy-looking vase with a lid in his other hand.

He paused for a moment, looking me in the eyes. Then, he nodded to himself as if answering his own question. Then he asked if my dad was home.

I turned around and yelled, "Dad! There's a salesman at the door for you."

I looked back at the man and stared straight into his eyes. He stared back. He didn't know it, but I had started a staring contest. We stared each other in the eyes for a good thirty seconds. Then I blinked. I was frustrated that I lost, especially since the guy didn't even know it was a competition.

Dad finally made his way down the stairs. He put his hand on my shoulder as he stood beside me at the open door.

"Hi, mister. I'm not interested in whatever you're selling," Dad said in an annoyed tone.

Dad began to close the door, but the mystery man began speaking.

"Oh. I'm not selling anything, sir. My name is Stan Truman. I'm a lawyer."

Dad looked at me with nervous eyes. He squeezed my shoulder tightly with his hand. Then he told me to go play. I grumbled something under my breath to show my frustration that I was being cut out of the conversation. I ran out the back door and snuck to the front corner of the house. I hoped to catch a glimpse of what was happening on the porch, but I couldn't see or hear anything.

That's when a sneaky idea came into my mind. We had a giant oak tree on the side of the house. One of its massive branches stretched over the house, and part of it hung over the uncovered front porch where the lawyer was still standing.

I climbed that big oak quickly and stealthily. I inched my way down the long branch as quietly as possible. I was like a ninja. I didn't stop until I was right over the lawyer's head.

Neither my dad nor the lawyer had any clue that I was up above listening in. I could hear their conversation perfectly. I missed a little bit of what had already been said, but I made it just in time for the lawyer to get to the good stuff.

"Sir, I know my visit has come unannounced, and I sincerely apologize. I regretfully bring a bit of bad news," he explained.

Stan paused and bowed his head. I think he was trying to create a dramatic effect.

"I'm here to inform you that William Halveston Grant has passed on from this life," Stan said solemnly as he handed my dad the fancy vase.

My dad looked at the vase with big, grossed-out eyes.

"Whoa! Is this an urn full of this guy's ashes? I'm sorry, but I have no idea who you are even talking about. I don't know anyone by that name," Dad said as he shoved the vase back into the lawyer's hands.

The lawyer briefly looked down at the urn, then smiled, "I think you probably knew him as Grandpa Willie."

He put the urn back into my dad's hands.

"Oh, Grandpa Willie!" Dad said with surprise in his voice.

"I never actually met my Grandpa Willie. My dad, Cliff, got into a big fight with him when I was just a toddler. They never spoke to each other again. I grew up without ever even meeting Grandpa Willie," Dad explained.

"Yes, yes. I know the story. It was a shame, really. Your Grandpa Willie was quite the character. You would have liked him. One of Willie's biggest regrets was that fight with your father," explained Stan.

"I bet. So, what does his death have to do with me? Why are you here? And why are you giving me his ashes?" Dad asked bluntly.

"I'm sorry, sir. Let me get straight to it. Your grandpa left a very detailed will," replied Stan.

"Did Grandpa Willie leave me something in his will?" Dad asked innocently.

"No. He didn't just leave you something. He left you everything," Stan said.

He paused again as he seemed to enjoy the surprised look on my dad's face.

"But there is one tiny condition," Stan stated nervously.

Dad's eyebrows raised with suspicion. He turned his head slightly to the left.

"What does 'everything' mean? And what is the one condition?" asked Dad.

"Everything… is a tremendous fortune. More money than you can imagine. Grandpa Willie was a very, very rich man," Stan said while nodding his head repeatedly.

My jaw dropped as I heard him say "fortune." I put my right hand in the air and started pumping it up and down excitedly. We were going to be rich! We were going to be filthy rich!

Unfortunately, that is when I slipped and fell out of the tree. Luckily, I landed right on top of the lawyer, so it didn't hurt much….

As the lawyer and I hit the ground with a thud, his briefcase flew into the air and burst open, sending papers flying everywhere.

I climbed off of the lawyer and started picking up the loose papers. A slight breeze made the papers dance as I reached for them. My dad helped Stan to his feet and began apologizing for what I had done. My dad was very practiced in apologizing for my bad behavior.

"I'm glad you gave the urn full of ashes to my dad. Imagine the vase hitting the concrete and breaking open. His ashes would have gone everywhere," I laughed nervously.

I put my head down and continued to gather the papers fluttering in the wind. Then, a Polaroid picture caught my eye. It was a picture of an old, spooky-looking mansion.

"Holy moly, this place is creepy! What is this a picture of?" I blurted out.

"That, young man, is the one condition," explained Stan.

I stopped gathering papers. I looked straight into the lawyer's eyes. He broke our gaze and looked straight at my dad with some intensity. He cleared his throat with a nervous cough.

"The one condition to inherit the fortune is to move your family to Eerie Hollow and make Grandpa Willie's mansion your permanent home."

The lawyer stepped closer to me. He bent over so that our eyes were at the same level. He snatched the papers I had picked up right out of my hand. Then he leaned in closer and whispered into my ear where Dad couldn't hear him.

"McKay, the adventure of a lifetime, is found within the walls of this mansion. Your Great-Grandpa Willie believed that you are the ONE," Stan said with excitement in his whisper.

Then he stood back up and acted as if he hadn't whispered anything into my ear.

"If we could go inside, I would be more than happy to answer all of your questions," offered Stan.

My dad looked like he was in complete shock. He looked at me and then at Stan. Dad looked a little flustered.

"Eerie Hollow is where I was born. My dad lived with Grandpa Willie in that mansion before the big argument. When I was older, I mentioned Eerie Hollow once, and Dad got really upset. He forbade me from ever talking about that place ever again."

Then Dad shook his head thoughtfully, "I'm sorry. Where are my manners? Of course, you can come inside."

He opened the door, and we all entered the living room together. The lawyer looked around at our walls as we walked into the house. Giant whitetail mounts lined the living room area of our relatively small home. My dad and mom were pretty amazing hunters, and they proudly displayed their buck memories for all to see.

"You are a hunter?" Stan asked my dad.

"Yes, we all love to hunt," Dad replied humbly.

Dad walked over to the back door and hollered outside for my mom to come inside. Mom was working out in her garden. While Dad was at the back door, the lawyer asked me if any of the bucks on the wall were mine.

"Yep. All of them!" I said with the most confident look on my face.

Stan's eyebrows raised high in response to my bold claim. Mom and Dad walked into the room holding hands like they always did.

The lawyer looked at them and said, "You must be very proud of your son! He claims that every single one of these bucks are his...."

Mom looked at me with daggers in her eyes and yelled, "McKay! What have I told you about lying? Go to your room right now!"

I put my head down and made my way up the stairs. When I was about halfway up, I looked down at the lawyer. Stan was looking back at me. He smiled a toothy smile. Then he spoke to me again—this time for all to hear.

"Young man, there are bucks so big in Eerie Hollow that they are worth dying over...."

Chapter 3

Sneaking Around

We had quite a discussion after Stan left. Mom didn't want to leave her friends or her garden. Dad would have to quit the job that he had worked at for over fifteen years. Dad also worried about my Grandpa Cliff's negative feelings about Eerie Hollow. I guess there was some real trauma there.

But on the other hand, living in a mansion and having all the money we could ever spend was quite appealing, if you know what I mean.

In the end, Mom, Dad, and I decided, as a family, to move to Eerie Hollow together. We would live in the mansion where Dad had taken his first steps as a toddler. Dad was more than a little nervous about telling Grandpa Cliff that we would be returning to Eerie Hollow, but that wouldn't stop us from turning the spooky mansion into our new home. I mean, who would turn down a vast fortune? We're not dumb dumbs.

In hindsight, it was pretty strange that the lawyer knew me by name. It was also quite odd that Great-Grandpa Willie thought I was the "ONE." What in the world did that even mean? The one what? The one best-looking boy in the world? Well, ya, obviously... but what did he really mean? I had never met the guy, and he declared I was the one. Whatever.

Things moved quickly after we made our final decision, and within a week, our moving truck was full. We made the long drive to Eerie Hollow. Now, here we were, unpacking our few things into a house with twelve bedrooms.

I felt a bit of culture shock as I looked around the mansion. It was absolutely amazing. The walls were tall and ornate. Large paintings of wildlife hung proudly throughout the mansion. White, beautiful pillars rose from the floor to the ceiling. I looked over at the large granite fireplace.

A fancy painting of Great-Grandpa Willie hung over the fireplace mantle. I stood in front of the painting and stared. I was first drawn to his eyes. They were full of kindness with a hint of mischief. He wore round, wire-rimmed glasses that sat on the bridge of his nose. Deep wrinkles covered his forehead. A long white handlebar mustache partially covered his big, playful smile. His white hair was a bit wild, in my opinion, almost like he had just gotten out of bed. I nodded to myself. This was definitely a man that I wished I could have had the chance to meet. He looked like a hoot of fun!

My parents had put Great-Grandpa Willie's urn full of ashes on the marble mantle under the painting. Part of me wanted to go and look inside the urn. I'd never seen a person's ashes before and wondered what they looked like, but I decided not to.

It took a lot of work to pick a bedroom with twelve options, but I found the perfect one. It was huge and even had a built-in hammock. The room had two king-sized beds, so Jack and I decided to share the bedroom while he visited. We figured being together would be more fun while he was here. You know, so we could have guy chats before going to bed. That sort of stuff.

I looked at Jack. He was sitting on a fancy chair, minding his own business. I was glad that he was here with me. I liked the idea of an adventure of a lifetime hiding within these walls and sharing that adventure with him. I decided that Jack and I would have to explore the mansion on our own that night after the adults went to bed. I was all about getting into some trouble... err... I mean adventure.

I have to be honest, though. It was nice knowing Uncle Dallas was here just in case this place was haunted. I mean, what kind of ghost would stick around with Uncle Dallas roaming the hallways?

For the rest of the day, we all worked hard unloading the moving truck. By the time the sun went down, I was definitely worn out, but Dad looked way more tired than I was. He stood up after dinner and declared to the room that he was going to bed. Mom agreed that was a good idea. She followed him to their new master bedroom, which was probably the size of our old house. Uncle Dallas stood up and stretched with a thunderous yawn. Then, he went upstairs to his room and left Jack and me alone at the table.

I looked over at Jack, raised my eyebrows, and said, "Are you ready to do some exploring?"

He looked at me with mischief in his eyes, "Absolutely, let's see what secrets this mansion is hiding."

Suddenly, the lights went out. My first thought was that it had to be ghosts. Then it hit me. It was Mom. She had a thing about turning lights off. Mom couldn't stand lights being on when no one was using them. I was sure it was her, but I don't think she realized she was leaving her son and nephew in the dark in an old, eerie mansion!

It was ink-black everywhere. I couldn't even see my hand in front of my face. I stood up from the table, and my chair fell behind me with a loud crash. I freaked out a little bit on the inside.

With the lights off, the mansion took on a new level of spookiness. The only light in the mansion came from the full moon shining through the old windows. Just our luck, a full moon for sure meant that the ghosts would be out and about. Luckily, I had a flashlight in my backpack. I pulled it out and turned it on. The beam of light shone directly on Jack's face.

He squinted and put his hands up to his eyes to protect them from the light, "McKay! Aim that thing somewhere else!"

"Oops... Sorry Jack. My bad," I chuckled.

I wasn't sorry, though. I had done that on purpose.

We started to snoop around. I shined my light on the grand staircase in front of us. It was a sight to behold. The entry to the stairs was at least twelve feet wide. The handrails that went up to the second floor were made out of dark walnut, just like the steps. There were fancy decorated posts at the head of the stairs that were topped with giant whitetail bucks carved out of solid wood. They were the same dark walnut color as the rest of the wooden staircase. The bucks faced each other. They had their heads down with their giant antlers leading the way as if they were ready to fight each other.

"I would love to see those studs fight," whispered Jack as we walked between the giant bucks to go up the stairs.

"You're not kidding," I replied.

I thought about how neat it would be to see these bucks fight in real life. The stairs creaked as we made our way up. I worried the loud creaks would alert my mom and dad to our snooping. After the first eight steps, the staircase split into two, wrapping around a giant bronze statue of a hunter that went down to the main floor. The statue must have been fifteen feet tall. The hunter stood proud. He looked down the barrel of an old muzzleloader as if he was about ready to take a shot. It was unreal.

A spider web made its way up from the hunter's nose down to the end of the barrel. The hunter looked like he was aiming at a giant buck in a massive painting at the top of the stairs.

"Look at that painting," I whisper-yelled to Jack.

I couldn't keep my excitement quiet, but I knew I would be in big trouble if I woke up my mom. She loves sleep more than ice cream, and she really loves ice cream.

"Let's check it out," Jack whispered back.

Jack went up the left side of the stairs, and I went up the right. Once we made it around the enormous statue, the staircase came back together for another eight steps to the second floor.

The painting on the wall at the top of the stairs was brilliant. The frame seemed to be made of solid silver, but it paled in comparison to the masterful painting. I had never seen anything like it. The painting wasn't smooth. The brushstrokes had depth. I could see each dash of color as if it were three-dimensional. I stood there with my mouth open, unable to pull my eyes away.

The main focus of the painting was a ginormous buck. He stood tall and confident. An eerie fog surrounded him and covered the bottom half of his legs, but his face and antlers were clear and sharp. His antlers were very unique. They were wider than most bucks that I had seen. He was probably twice the size of the bucks my parents had hanging on the wall of our old home.

His antlers were bone white. I counted the points. It looked like there were eighteen points total, but it was hard to be sure. Some of the points were hidden behind others. I wished I could turn the buck's antlers to get a better look.

The most exciting feature of the antlers was the double drop tines. Each side of the enormous rack had a point aimed downwards. The drop tine on his right side split into two, looking like a crawdad claw.

The hairs on my arm stood straight up as I looked into the buck's eyes. They were incredibly strange. They were a penetrating white. They almost seemed to glow as if he was a ghost among the living. I shook my head real quick to try to shake away the creepiness that I felt.

The scenery behind the buck was super interesting. A rock formation among the fog on the left side of the buck was pretty spooky-looking. I couldn't tell, really, but it almost looked like there was an opening in the rocks.

"Do you think that's a cave?" I asked Jack.

"It might be, but who cares," he replied.

Just the thought of a creepy cave gave me the chills. I hated small, tight spaces.

A couple of shoulder mounts hung to the left and right of the painting. The bucks were big, but nothing compared to the buck in the painting.

"Great-Grandpa Willie was definitely obsessed with hunting," I whispered to Jack.

"I'd say. It's too bad we didn't get to know him while he was alive. I bet he would have taken us hunting!"

I nodded my head in agreement. We continued to look around as we tip-toed past my parent's room as quietly as possible.

To the right of their room was a long, dark hallway. I shined my flashlight down the hall. My heart jumped as I saw glowing eyes. My first instinct was to run, but I didn't want to look like a scaredy cat in front of Jack. I couldn't show him that I was scared at all.

We both walked bravely towards the glowing eyes, but to my profound relief, they were just the glass eyes of a full-body bobcat mount. It looked old. I wondered what kind of memory this bobcat held for Great-Grandpa Willie.

Then, suddenly, we heard the creak of a door opening slowly behind us. My heart jumped out of my chest. I shined my light towards the sound. A huge groan came from the doorway. Jack and I instinctively grabbed onto each other. We both began to shake violently. A humongous figure stepped into the dark hallway....

Chapter 4

Bigfoot

The first thing I saw was a giant, hairy foot. It took a slow step towards us. My flashlight lit up its dark, hairy leg. My hand shook so hard that I dropped the flashlight onto the hallway floor. Thankfully, the beam of light lit up our escape route.

"Run!" I yelled to Jack.

We both turned and ran down the hall. We turned the corner. A fancy door with an X carved into it was at the end of a short hallway. Jack and I scrambled to get to the door to make our escape.

The brass door knob on the fancy door was large and ornate. I frantically tried opening it, but the door was locked. We could hear the creature's steps coming around the corner. We dropped to the ground and screamed at the top of our lungs, awaiting a gruesome death. But what came next was more terrifying than anything I could ever possibly describe.

The figure at the end of the hallway reached out and flipped the light switch on the wall. The light illuminated the hairy monster.

To our absolute horror, it was Uncle Dallas standing in front of us, nearly naked. His only clothing was a pair of white boxer shorts covered in red hearts. He held his big hairy belly as it bounced up and down with his laughter.

"What are you two doing on the floor? Did you think I was a monster or something?" Uncle Dallas said as he belly laughed again.

He laughed even harder, and then he laughed some more. He couldn't stop laughing at us. It was embarrassing, to say the least.

"Uncle Dallas! I thought you were Bigfoot! You are a seriously hairy man. Has anyone ever told you that before?" I hollered out.

"Dad! Put some clothes on before my eyes start bleeding!" Jack shouted.

Jack covered his eyes with his hands to protect them from the terrifying scene. Then, as if things weren't already embarrassing enough, my parents came around the corner to see where all the screaming had come from. Dad and Mom walked past Dallas and saw us sitting on the ground.

"What in the world is going on here?" Mom asked as she picked my flashlight off of the floor and shined it in our faces.

It felt like the FBI was interrogating us. Actually, the FBI would have been less intimidating than my mom was....

"Nothing, we just thought Dallas was Bigfoot, that's all," I replied.

Mom shined the light on Dallas's hairy body and grinned.

"Dallas, when did you get this hairy? It looks like you're wearing a fur coat. Do you have to brush your chest hair to keep it from tangling?"

Dallas brushed through his thick chest hair with his fingers and said, "The older I get, the hairier I get. It keeps me nice and toasty up there in the Alaskan tundra."

We all started laughing together. The look on Dallas' face was pretty funny. Then Mom's attention turned back onto us.

"What were you doing sneaking around with this flashlight?" she asked suspiciously.

"Funny story, Mom. Umm. When you went to bed, you turned off all the lights in this spooky mansion and left Jack and me in the dark. We were just trying to find our bedroom when your Sasquatch brother scared the living daylights out of us!" I replied innocently.

"Hmmm. Interesting story. You two know your bedroom is on the first floor, right? You were up to no good, weren't you? Go to bed," she commanded.

Jack and I stood up slowly and walked by Uncle Dallas and my parents. We kept our eyes on the floor and did not make eye contact with any of them. We retraced our steps down the hall and passed by the painting at the top of the stairs. I looked into the buck's white, glowing eyes. It felt like he was watching me. Shivers went down my spine. I shook my head quickly, then hurried down the stairs to my new bedroom.

"Man, that was embarrassing. I can't believe your dad is so hairy," I said.

"No kidding. I'm just glad it was him and not the real Bigfoot," he replied.

He paused for a moment and clarified, "Although, even if it was Bigfoot, I'm pretty sure I could have taken him on. I mean, if I can scare a grizzly away, I could totally scare Bigfoot, too," Jack bragged.

I rolled my eyes at his boastful claim and said, "Are you sure it wasn't the pistol that scared the grizzly away?"

Jack didn't answer. He pretended like he was already asleep. I knew he wasn't sleeping though, because he snores like a banshee when he sleeps. I closed my eyes and quickly fell asleep.

Chapter 5

The Festival

The following day, I woke up to the smell of bacon—my favorite! I ran out of my bedroom and straight to the kitchen. Mom, Dad, and Jack were already eating, and Dallas was cooking.

"Hey McKay! Good morning, sleepy head!" Dad exclaimed.

"Did I sleep in? What's going on?" I asked.

"We thought we'd get the day started early. We wanted to get some unpacking done and then go explore the town. What do you think?" Mom asked.

"I like how you think!" I replied.

We spent most of the day unpacking and making the mansion feel more like home. Mom and Dad even hung their big buck mounts in the living room. By the time we were ready to go, it was evening. We grabbed our jackets and opened our front door. Our mansion was at the very end of Main Street of Eerie Hollow. A light fog filled the street. I could see why they named this place Eerie Hollow.

I kicked up some colored leaves that had fallen onto the cracked sidewalk. This time of the year was my favorite. There was something special about how the cool, crisp fall air felt on my face. It also meant I'd be deer hunting in the woods before I knew it. I thought about what the lawyer, Stan Truman, had said to me the day he visited us.

"Young man, there are bucks so big in Eerie Hollow that they are worth dying over...."

Boy, I sure hope he was right, although I couldn't imagine someone actually dying over a buck. That would be crazy....

I couldn't wait to get out into the woods, especially since Jack was with me. We would definitely be shooting some giants this fall. Just then, Jack hit the back of my head with his hand and knocked me out of my daydreaming. I shot him a confused, angry look.

"Are you seeing what I'm seeing?" Jack asked out loud.

I had no idea what he was talking about.

"What do you mean?" I responded in a frustrated manner as I rubbed the back of my head.

"Every single one of these houses along the street has the same creepy decorations. Look!"

I looked up and down the street. He was right. It was so strange.

"What in the world," I muttered out loud.

Every porch had a dressed-up plastic skeleton sitting on a rocking chair. The skeletons were all dressed the same way. The skulls were covered with a brown trapper hat. You know the kind of hat that has fur on the insides, and the side of the hat can fold down to cover your ears? Then, each skeleton wore a red plaid flannel shirt and dirty blue jean overalls. Interestingly enough, the skeletons were not wearing boots. The bony feet were covered in red wool socks and nothing more.

Each skeleton held its left hand close to its mouth. It looked like they might have been eating something, but I couldn't see what was actually going on. The skeleton held a kerosene lantern at head height in its other hand. The lantern was the only light on each porch, and it eerily lit up the skeleton's face.

"Dad, what is going on here? Why does every house have a skeleton dressed up like that?" I asked, feeling a little bit frightened on the inside.

He looked at me and shrugged his shoulders.

"I have no idea, son," he replied honestly, looking just as confused as me.

We continued to walk cautiously towards the business section of Eerie Hollow. Once we entered the town center, we saw a giant banner stretch across Main Street. The words on the banner said:

**The Festival of
The Phantom of Eerie Hollow**

I looked at Jack, but his eyes were fixed on something in the distance. My heart started to beat a little faster. The fog seemed to be getting thicker as I looked around the creepy town. Through the dreary mist, I saw lights floating about five feet in the air. I felt a slight panic inside my chest. This was unnatural, for sure.

I strained my eyes to try to see more clearly what it was that I was seeing. One of the floating lights was getting closer to us. Then, slowly, the light illuminated the hands and body of a strange-looking person. He carried a kerosene lantern at head height, just like the ones I saw on the porches.

Chapter 6

Crazy Carl

The hairs on my neck stood tall, and my breathing got erratic. I moved closer to my Uncle Dallas, hoping he would protect me from the horrifying scene before me. As I looked closer, I realized that every one of the lights was a lantern carried by someone dressed the same way: a brown trapper hat, a red plaid flannel shirt, blue jean overalls, and red wool socks with no boots....

Suddenly, I heard the creepiest musical sounds carry through the wind. I had heard that whiny sound before but couldn't figure out what was creating it.

The first figure holding a lantern slowly passed by. He didn't even look at us. He walked like a zombie or something with his eyes straight forward. He lifted his left hand to his mouth and made a musical sound. It was a harmonica! That's when I realized that the skeletons on the porches were not eating something. They were holding a harmonica to their lips.

Then, in unison, everyone holding a lantern sang a simple, depressing song while they wandered aimlessly in the street. It was probably the spookiest thing I've ever witnessed. The song went like this:

Oh, Phantom of the woods, tell me your tale,
Of ancient secrets and nights so pale.
Lost in the mist, your presence is near,
Losing you is my ultimate fear.

Through tangled vines and whisper of trees,
The Phantom wanders, a silent breeze.
Eyes like stars, piercing the night,
I cannot seem to win this fight.

Though I may fear the dark's embrace,
The Phantom beckons from this place.
But in its realm, there's solace found,
A sanctuary where peace resounds.

I was so confused. The words of the song made my heart feel depressed. I truly felt sad for some reason.

Then I looked up and saw a tall, gangly man walking towards us with his lantern held high. He was dressed like the rest, but there was something familiar about this man. I watched him closely as he got closer. He was coming straight at us! The lantern's light illuminated his face. It was familiar, but I couldn't seem to remember where I had seen it before. Then, it hit me like a baseball bat to the forehead.

"Stan!" I yelled out.

The man stopped in his tracks and looked down at me. He put the harmonica to his lips and blew. Then he sang the sad song again with the rest of the lantern bearers.

When he finished the song, he looked me straight in the eyes without blinking. Then, a grin slowly spread across his mouth. It was like he snapped out of a trance or something.

"McKay! I'm so glad you and your family are here! I was hoping you'd get a chance to see the performance!" said Stan.

"Stan, what in the world is going on here? This is probably the spookiest thing I've ever seen!" I exclaimed.

"What do you mean 'performance'?" Dad asked bluntly.

Stan smiled big and pointed around the town.

"It's all a big performance! We're reenacting the town's famous ghost story. Have you never heard of The Phantom of Eerie Hollow?" Stan looked shocked, as if he couldn't believe that Dad hadn't heard the story.

"No. Never," Dad replied.

Stan's eyes widened in disbelief as he shook his head oddly.

"Really? That's shocking. Well, you are in for a treat. People from all over the country come to Eerie Hollow to see the reenactment. Many of the town's citizens participate in one way or another. Every day for a month, we take turns dressing up like Ol' Crazy Carl and walk the streets singing his song. After this performance, everyone meets in the woods to hear the spooky ghost story. Then, everyone returns to the fairground to play games and eat food. It's my favorite time of the year. Tonight happens to be a foggy night, so everything is extra eerie. Would you like to go to the woods to hear the ghost story?" Stan asked all of us.

Mom looked at Dad, Dad looked at Dallas, Dallas looked at Jack, Jack looked at me, and I looked at Mom. We all nodded together, and then Mom spoke for all of us.

"Absolutely. Is it free, or do we buy tickets or something?"

Stan smiled his toothy smile and reached into his pocket, and pulled out five tickets.

"You have to buy tickets for the ghost story and the festival. But, lucky for you, I have five tickets with your names on them."

He handed out the tickets one by one. He paused when he got to me. He smiled his toothy grin, then leaned down to my height and handed me a ticket with his right hand. He secretly dropped something heavy into my jacket pocket with his left hand.

Then he whispered into my ear, "McKay, this will help you find that adventure I promised you."

He stood up tall and told us he needed to get back to acting. Instantly, he got back in character and walked past us, singing the sad song with the rest of the Crazy Carls.

I reached into my pocket and felt the object that Stan had quietly given me. It was metal. It felt like it was about three inches long. I turned away from my family and pulled it out to see what it was. As I pulled it out of my pocket, I felt the hair stand on the back of my neck once more.

Chapter 7

Ghost Story

A smile broke across my face as my eyes fell upon the object Stan Truman had secretly given me. It was a key, but different from the typical kind of key you would use to open your front door's deadbolt. It was at least three inches long and made of pitted black metal. It looked old, almost ancient. The handle portion had a circle with an X through the center. The shaft of the key was rod-like and bare. The end of the key had blunt, jagged teeth. I was in awe. I had never seen a key like this before. I wondered what the key could possibly open. Would it open a lock on a chest of gold? Or was it meant to open a safe? Maybe it would open a room with a treasure map?

"McKay! What are you looking at?" interrupted Jack.

I quickly returned the mystery key to my pocket and pretended to look at the ticket instead. I wasn't ready to share the key with Jack.

"Oh, just looking at the name on the ticket that Stan gave to us. So... is this Crazy Carl guy The Phantom of Eerie Hollow?" I ventured.

Jack scrunched his face as if he was thinking hard and responded, "I guess so. I don't know who else it could be. I bet we will find more out in the woods when they tell the ghost story."

I looked up and noticed that all the Crazy Carls had gathered in an open area in the center of town, where a stage had been set up. They all held their lanterns high to cast their light on Stan. He stood on a stage all by himself. He began to speak loudly.

"We will now head deep into the woods of Eerie Hollow. Hold on tightly to your loved ones, and keep your eyes wide open. Before Ol' Crazy Carl disappeared forever, he was known for his trickster behavior. Don't let him get you!" Stan expressed with his toothy grin.

Then, all the actors playing Crazy Carl formed a line and invited the tourists to walk with them. Stan waved us over to walk by the light of his lantern. I tried to talk to him, but he was back to playing his character. He didn't say a single word to us. No one spoke. It was absolutely silent as we all walked deep into the haunted forest.

We crested a large hill after a long hike through the dark woods. I looked down the hill and saw a wooden stage at the bottom with a fire pit in front. I then realized that seats had been dug out of the hillside. Flagstone had been fitted perfectly into the hill to make an amphitheater. It was pretty impressive, to say the least.

Stan led us to a great place to sit right in the middle of the hill. Then he left us to go to the stage with the rest of the guides. The stage was completely dark until Stan put his lantern down at the front edge of the stage. A slender man with a dark, bushy mustache appeared in the lantern's light. He wore a plain white button-up shirt. A pair of black suspenders held up his brown khaki pants.

The lantern's flickering light cast an eerie glow. The light danced across the man's face, distorting his true appearance. He started to breathe very deeply. We watched as his chest puffed slowly in and out. He began to breathe so loudly that every soul in the audience could hear his deep, fear-filled breaths. With every deep, hoarse breath, my heart beat a little faster. It was downright spooky.

Then he spoke. His voice trembled as he began to relate the tale of The Phantom of Eerie Hollow.

"Carl... Carl... Carl...."

The mustache man said slowly and gravely.

"Carl was loved by all who knew him. He was known for his love of life and playful personality. The children of the town all adored him. In fact, I was one of those children many, many moons ago..."

He put his hand on his chest, revealing that he was a real-life witness to Carl's life.

"Carl was the kind of man that could do no wrong. There was something about his bright green eyes that made you feel cared about and loved. He split his time between his love of painting and cheering Eerie Hollow's children up with his small, playful tricks."

He paused for a second to clarify what he had said.

"You know, innocent tricks... like switching your Grandpa's coffee with orange juice when Grandpa wasn't looking. He'd look over at you and wink while you both waited to see Grandpa's reaction to the sweet orange juice. Then, when Grandpa spit out the juice, we would all laugh together."

He laughed out loud. Then he nodded to himself.

"Those were fun times...."

The man's bushy mustache gave way to a smile. He looked sincerely happy as if he was genuinely reliving that exact memory.

"Then, one day, he went hunting out in these woods right behind me. Oh boy, the man sure loved to hunt and was good at it, too. No buck could outsmart him. He always seemed to harvest the biggest buck in town every single year."

The storyteller raised his hands above his head, spreading his fingers to show how big those bucks were.

"I remember the opening day of rifle season that year as if it were yesterday. Carl came back from his opening morning hunt excited as any man had ever been. He burst into our classroom during school. You see, my fifth-grade teacher was Carl's twin brother. They were super close, if I remember correctly. They did just about everything together. I guess Carl just couldn't wait to tell his brother about the magnificent buck he had seen that day. He whooped and hollered and told us all about this giant buck he had seen. Twice as big as any buck he had ever taken."

This time, the older man put his hands above his head and extended his arms as far as he could to show how big the antlers were on this unique buck.

"Oh man, was Carl excited! We all laughed so hard when Carl grabbed a couple of yardsticks and pretended that they were his antlers. He got down on his hands and knees and went around the classroom, pretending to be a giant buck. He grunted and wheezed while he pawed at the ground. Carl went over to our teacher and rubbed the yardsticks against his legs as if he was raking his giant antlers on a tree."

Stan came onto the stage pretending to be Carl. He was holding two yardsticks. Stan got on his hands and knees. He grunted and wheezed. He pawed at the ground and made his way over to the storyteller. Stan held the two yardsticks up to his head and raked the legs of the storyteller like a buck rubbing a tree. Everyone in the audience laughed at the sight. Then Stan stood up and walked off the stage.

"Carl promised us all that we would get to see the ginormous buck because he'd be bringing him home soon enough. He waved goodbye to us children, but as he left the classroom, he exchanged the chalk sitting on the chalkboard with a baby carrot. We laughed our heads off when our teacher tried to write on the chalkboard with that carrot! It smeared across the chalkboard, leaving a streak of wetness. Even our teacher had to laugh at the funny prank."

The slender man chuckled as he recalled that moment. Then, the laugh stopped as abruptly as it came. His face changed in an instant. Pure agony appeared on the mustache man's face.

"Sadly, that was the last time any of us ever saw Carl happy. That was the last funny prank we ever saw him play. He became entirely, totally, absolutely, and utterly obsessed with that giant buck. He would leave early in the morning for the woods and disappear for weeks. I remember when he came back to town after his first prolonged stint in the woods. I saw crazy brewing in his eyes. He ranted about this Phantom Buck. He complained that he could not harvest him no matter how hard he tried. He claimed that the buck was not of this world. In the darkness, the buck's eyes glowed a bright white. Carl then told us he named the buck The Phantom of Eerie Hollow.

I looked over at Jack, and he looked at me with big eyes.

"Jack, I thought Carl was The Phantom of Eerie Hollow?" I whispered.

Jack shrugged and put his index finger to his lips to tell me to be quiet.

The mustache man continued, "Carl, then disappeared in his house. Not a soul saw him, not even his twin brother, for several days. The townsfolk began to worry about him. Carl was all that we could talk about. Then, one gloomy day, he emerged from his home looking ghostly white and wearing the same clothes as he wore before he had disappeared."

Stan walked back onto the stage at this moment and stood there. The storyteller pointed to Stan's clothing.

"A brown trapper hat. A red plaid flannel shirt. Filthy jean overalls..."

He paused for a moment before he pointed at Stan's feet.

"And red wool socks with no boots... I remember working up the courage to ask Carl where his boots were. He looked me in the eyes and hissed, 'The Phantom can hear my footsteps when I wear boots. Why would I wear boots if he could hear my boots? I'll go barefoot if that's what it takes to harvest The Phantom of Eerie Hollow. Leave me alone, kid!' Then he walked straight into these woods once more, not to be seen for another couple of weeks."

The storyteller shook his head from side to side as if in deep emotional pain. Tears began to well up in his eyes.

"The last night that any of us ever saw him was during our fall pumpkin festival. He came out of these woods with a lantern while we enjoyed the festivities. He walked down the center of the festival with his eyes staring straight ahead as if he were in a trance. He played a few notes on his harmonica and sang his depressing song."

The mustached man began to sing the words to Carl's song. All the Crazy Carl actors came onto the stage and accompanied him in perfect harmony. Chills shot through my body as they sang. The music filled the forest air.

Oh, Phantom of the woods, tell me your tale,
Of ancient secrets and nights so pale.
Lost in the mist, your presence is near,
Losing you is my ultimate fear.

Through tangled vines and whisper of trees,
The Phantom wanders, a silent breeze.
Eyes like stars, piercing through the night,
I cannot seem to win this fight.

Though I may fear the dark's embrace,
The Phantom beckons in this place.
But in its realm, there's solace found,
A sanctuary where peace resounds.

The words of the song burned into my heart. I found myself tearing up. I wiped my eyes. I felt so bad for this Carl person. I didn't understand why I felt such a strong emotion for this person I didn't know.

The storyteller continued, "Crazy Carl, as he was now known to the town, slowly made his way home and sat down on his porch for the last time. He rocked in his chair, holding his kerosene lamp at eye level, as he stared into the distance. He played his sad song on the harmonica. You may have noticed how every house down Main Street decorates their porch with this depressing scene."

The slender man bowed his head in remembrance of that moment in time. The forest was silent again for a moment before he began speaking.

"Down at the end of Main Street, a couple of the most degenerate citizens of Eerie Hollow stumbled out of the "Eerie Pub" that cursed night. I won't name names since they regrettably still reside here in Eerie Hollow... but I will tell you that they are brothers. A tall brother and a round brother."

The storyteller raised his right hand when he mentioned the tall brother. Then, he extended both arms out to the side when he mentioned the round brother.

"These boys decided they'd pay poor Ol' Crazy Carl a visit. They stumbled down the road until they reached Carl's porch."

At this moment, the storyteller stepped slowly off the stage into the darkness. Stan brought out a rocking chair and grabbed his lantern from the front of the stage. He sat down and held the lantern at eye level, playing a few short notes on a harmonica. He was dressed like Crazy Carl.

Then, two other actors made their way onto the stage. One of the actors had platform shoes that made him a foot taller than he would have been without them. The other actor had stuffed his clothes with pillows to make himself appear rounder. They obviously played the role of the tall and round degenerate brothers that the storyteller had introduced. They stumbled over to where Stan was sitting, playing the role of Carl, and started a dialogue.

"Hey Crazy Carl! How does it feel to be the town's loon?" the round man hollered with a laugh.

"Don't you know there ain't no buck with white eyes out in the woods?" added the tall brother.

"You're hallucinating, man. You're seeing things that ain't there," retorted the round man.

"Ya, you're a sandwich short of a picnic," stated the tall one.

"Ha ha ha! You're a brick shy of a full load," laughed the round man.

"You've done lost your marbles," added the tall man as he pulled marbles out of his pocket and dropped them on Carl's head.

We heard the marbles hit the stage after they bounced off Carl's head. My heart broke at the sight of Carl being bullied by these awful men. Then, suddenly, the actors froze in place as the storyteller returned to the stage and stood behind the actors.

He opened his mouth and said, "That's when Crazy Carl stood up and pushed past the drunken bullies."

Stan stood up and pushed past the brothers.

"He marched down Main Street silently, all the way to the town center."

Stan marched in place on the stage silently, as if he was Carl walking down Main Street.

"He climbed onto the stage in the center of the Pumpkin Festival."

Stan pretended to walk upstairs onto a stage.

The mustache man continued, "Carl held his lantern high for a moment, casting its light onto the crowd before aggressively slamming the lantern down onto the wooden stage. Flames shot to the sky, surrounding Carl on every side."

Stan reared back and threw his lantern down into the fire pit in front of the stage. It must have been doused with gasoline because fire erupted from the ground and flew thirty feet into the air.

"From the heart of the flames, Crazy Carl made a promise for the whole town to hear!" yelled the story-teller.

Stan then shouted Carl's promise through the flames, "The Phantom Buck is real! He lives! I swear! I have stared into his glowing, white eyes. I vow to never return to this town without The Phantom of Eerie Hollow in my arms!"

Then Stan hissed Carl's infamous curse upon the town, "And if I never return.... Know this: I will haunt this town like the Phantom has haunted me. I will be your Phantom. You'll never be able to forget me. I'll be burned into the memory of this town, and on cool fall nights, you will hear me as the wind blows. Mark my words... I will haunt you...."

Then Stan jumped off the stage and disappeared into the woods just like Carl had done all those years ago...."

Chapter 8

Calling Me

The storyteller was now alone on the stage. He finished his story by saying, "We never saw Crazy Carl in the flesh again, but his presence has forever been felt. No man or woman has ever seen the giant, white-eyed buck that Carl named The Phantom of Eerie Hollow. But all of you that hear my voice tonight... know that... in this town... Carl is the true Phantom of Eerie Hollow."

The mustache man paused for dramatic effect, then continued, "Men have claimed to see his figure in the dark forest in the fall. The sound of his harmonica has been heard in the woods by all who dare to enter Carl's deer hunting grounds. He has haunted this town for decades with tricks and pranks and will continue to haunt us until he comes back with his Phantom Buck."

Jack and I looked at each other. We nodded as our question about who the Phantom was had been clarified.

"Carl and the white-eyed buck both play the role of The Phantom of Eerie Hollow," I whispered.

Then, the slender, mustached man pulled out a harmonica. He blew a few creepy notes and sang the song by himself one last time.

Oh, Phantom of the woods, tell me your tale,
Of ancient secrets and nights so pale.
Lost in the mist, your presence is near,
Losing you is my ultimate fear.

Through tangled vines and whisper of trees,
The Phantom wanders, a silent breeze.
Eyes like stars, piercing through the night,
I cannot seem to win this fight.

Though I may fear the dark's embrace,
The Phantom beckons in this place.
But in its realm, there's solace found,
A sanctuary where peace resounds.

Then, when the song's last word had left his lips, the actors doused the fire with water. Thick black smoke rose from the ashes, leaving us all in complete darkness.

No one moved. We all sat there in complete silence. Then, a slight breeze fell over the crowd. It carried a distant harmonica sound from the deep, dark, haunted woods. The whole crowd gasped. A woman in the crowd a few rows in front of me screamed at the top of her lungs, "It's Crazy Carl!" She trampled people as she tried to escape the haunted woods.

Her fear was contagious as others began to scream and run back towards town. Mom, Dad, Dallas, and Jack all stood up calmly and watched the crazy scene unfold. Jack had a smirk on his face as he watched everyone freak out. I, on the other hand, couldn't move. I sat there helpless in my seat, staring into the deep, dark forest of Eerie Hollow.

I don't know how to describe what I felt, but it was as if the sound of the harmonica was really Carl. He was calling to me to find him and bring him home. Suddenly, my Dad yanked on my arm and broke me out of my trance.

He looked down at me and said, "Son, let's go. It's over."

"Dad, did you hear that harmonica?" I asked.

"Of course. We all did. It was a great way for them to end the ghost story. No wonder people come here from all over. That was a top-notch, spooky experience," explained Dad.

"Are you saying that one of the actors played the harmonica?" I inquired.

"McKay, of course, it was an actor. You didn't actually think it was Crazy Carl? Did you?"

He laughed as he pulled me to my feet.

"Oh, uh, of course not, Dad. Umm. I'm not that gullible," I replied with a fake smile.

I tried not to let him see the truth in my eyes. Dad may have thought it was staged, but I wasn't so sure....

We all walked up the hill and made our way back to town. Jack and Dallas were laughing as they walked. They found the ghost story quite thrilling, and loved the fire spectacle at the end. On the other hand, I couldn't shake the feeling that Carl was calling out to me to free him. My mind would not let go of that feeling. As we walked back to the town, I replayed the story repeatedly in my head. There had to be more. There had to be....

We finally made it back to the festival through the dark fog, and I was glad we did. The festival was incredible! There were lots of booths with yummy foods. We filled up on buck-shaped cookies and bought a chocolate "Phantom Buck" cake to take home.

They even had hot chocolate with deer-shaped marshmallows. Uncle Dallas bought himself a coffee and took a big drink. His eyes got big as he spit it out all over the grass! They gave him orange juice instead of coffee- an obvious tribute to when Carl was a beloved town citizen. I think Carl would have been so much fun to be around before he went looney!

As we walked around the festival, we found a ton of shooting games. Most games had a massive buck with white eyes as the target. Jack and I got a little competitive at some of the booths, trying to prove to each other that we were the better shot. My favorite booth had real BB guns and two rows of buck-shaped metal targets that moved side to side.

The game's goal was to knock down all the bucks on your row before the other person knocked all of theirs down. The BB guns were lever action, so after each shot, we'd have to pull the lever action down to load another BB, then aim and shoot. It was tough, though, because if you missed, the booth attendant would push a button to stand one of your fallen bucks back up.

This booth attendant was a master at pitting two contestants against each other. He must have seen the pride in Jack and my eyes a mile away because, within the first minute of the first game, he had made Jack and me sworn enemies. The intensity level got pretty high, and before long, there was a huge crowd watching Jack and me play.

The final game we played was the most intense. Jack and I had each won five games, so we were tied. We decided that the eleventh game would be the tiebreaker. I heard the people in the crowd betting on who they thought would win. I couldn't let Jack beat me.

I looked over at Jack with narrow slits in my eyes. He looked back at me and curled his upper lip. We both took a deep breath as the booth attendant started the game. I shot fast and furious. My bucks were falling one after another. I got down to my last buck. I looked over at Jack, and he still had two bucks standing.

I wanted to win so badly that I rushed my shot. I heard the attendant yell, "Miss." He pushed a button, and one of my bucks stood back up. I reloaded quickly and knocked it right back down, but as I aimed at the final buck, the attendant stopped the game and declared Jack the winner.

I was so upset. I didn't even look at Jack. I just walked away with my head down. I shook my head in disgust. I would have won if I had not rushed my shot.

My parents saw my frustration and embarrassment, so they said it was time to go home. We all started the walk back to our spooky mansion together. I tried to ignore Jack. I didn't want to see the cocky look in his light blue eyes.

I fell behind the group and put my hands in my pockets. My fingers touched something cold and hard, and suddenly I remembered - the old key! I had forgotten all about it. I rubbed my thumb over the circle with the X in it. I ran my fingers over the jagged end of the key. Suddenly, I didn't care about losing anymore. My mind started racing with questions about this key.

"What could this key be for?" I whispered under my breath.

"Did Great-Grandpa Willie tell Stan to give it to me? Or did Stan have his own motives? Why did Stan give the key to me instead of to my parents? What kind of adventure did this key lead to?"

Chapter 9

Black X Key

That night, I did not get much sleep. My mind would not turn off. You know when you want to sleep, but your brain has other plans? All I could think about was poor Carl. Every time I almost drifted off to dreamland, a new thought popped into my head. Like, isn't it strange that Carl went crazy over a buck? I mean, I get the idea that you could get obsessed with a giant buck or get momentary buck fever, but I don't understand how someone could go entirely out of their mind forever over a buck.

There had to be more to the story than the storyteller shared at the festival. I tossed and turned that whole night, fighting off similar thoughts. Morning definitely came too quickly, that's for sure.

Mom and Dad called for me to get up and come to breakfast. I begrudgingly got out of bed and made my way to the kitchen. Everyone was talking about the spooky experience from the night before. While they were chatting, an idea hit me. How come Dad didn't know about The Phantom of Eerie Hollow? Wasn't he born here? Surely, Grandpa Cliff had mentioned something about the town's ghost story over the years.

"Dad, did you notice how shocked Stan looked when you said you had never heard of The Phantom of Eerie Hollow?"

"I did. It was kind of strange how Stan reacted, to be honest," Dad admitted.

"Did Grandpa Cliff never mention it? I mean, he lived here when you were born. You would think the ghost story would have at least come up over the years," I ventured.

"McKay, your Grandpa Cliff has strong, negative feelings about this place. I mean, when I called him and told him we were moving here, he hung up on me. He's normally a pretty level-headed man... I don't know what his deal is," Dad said as he shook his head in bewilderment.

Mom went over to Dad and hugged him. She gave me a look like I should drop the subject, so I did. I excused myself from the table and went back to my room. I went to the desk where I had stashed the old black key and pulled it out. I stared at it for a few moments, studying it. The circle with the X through it looked vaguely familiar, but I couldn't figure out where I had seen that shape before. That's when Jack burst into the room.

I turned around quickly and hid the key behind my back, but Jack knew that I was hiding something.

"What are you hiding from me? You have been acting weird. Tell me what it is. Tell me right now," he demanded.

I shook my head from side to side. He walked up to me and reached for my hand, that held the key behind my back. We started to wrestle over it. I held my hand closed as tightly as I could. Jack was pretty strong, but I wasn't going to give in. He pried at my hand until we both tripped and fell onto the floor. He landed on top of me, but I still wouldn't let go of the key. We were at a stalemate until he licked his finger and put it in my ear!

"Gross!" I yelled.

I wiped my ear from his disgusting spit. The key fell onto the floor with a thud. We both looked at it, and then Jack looked me directly in the eyes.

"Whoa! What an old-looking key. Neat! Where did you get it? What does it open?" he asked excitedly.

I huffed with a mix of exhaustion and frustration, "Stan gave it to me last night when he handed me the ticket. I don't know what it opens yet."

"I knew you were hiding something!" boasted Jack.

Jack picked up the key and analyzed it. He ran his fingers over it just like I did, and his light blue eyes lit up with excitement.

"I think I know what it opens," Jack said, lifting his eyebrows high.

"How do you know that?" I responded.

"The circle with the X in it. It looks exactly like that door that we tried to open. Remember when we were running away from my dad when we thought he was Bigfoot?"

"You're right! I knew I had seen that symbol before!" I said excitedly.

We both hopped up off the floor and opened the door to our room. We looked in both directions to see if any adults were around. We didn't see anyone, so we tiptoed down the hall and made our way to the giant staircase. We crept up the stairs as quietly as we could. I looked at the enormous bronze hunting sculpture as we passed by. It was indeed a work of art.

We passed by the painting of the double drop tine buck and turned the corner that led us past Uncle Dallas' room. We walked as quietly as we could past his door. We saw the stuffed bobcat at the end of the hallway. It wasn't nearly as spooky during the daytime. Then we rounded the corner to the hallway that led to the fancy door.

As the door came into view, our jaws dropped. It was so much more striking in the daylight! It was unlike any other door in the whole mansion. The door was expertly carved from top to bottom. I ran my fingers across the smooth, carved wood. A fancy border had been carved around the entire door. Then, in the center was a smooth, giant circle with an X in the middle.

I pulled out the key and held it in front of my eyes. I overlaid the key's symbol over the door's symbol. It was identical, just like Jack had thought. This had to be the door it opened.

I took the key and slid it perfectly into the large, brass door knob. I turned the key slowly and heard the lock click open.

I looked at Jack with excitement in my eyes. He looked back with a giant smile. I pulled the key out carefully. I put my hand on the doorknob. I closed my eyes for a moment in anticipation of the adventure that had been promised to me. I turned the knob to the right and slowly opened the door....

Chapter 10

The Painting

No, the room wasn't filled with treasure. It was just an office. A really, really fancy office. There was a large wooden desk that faced a big window that overlooked a pretty pond on the property. The walls were covered with bookshelves filled with old leather-bound books. The room smelled like leather. The desk was clean. It only had a simple white mug on it. When I looked closer, I saw that the mug had "Willie" printed on it.

"I'm guessing that this was Great-Grandpa Willie's office," I said.

I tried to show Jack the mug, but his attention was on a painting hanging high on the wall. He had a curious look on his face.

"Come check this out," Jack beckoned.

I walked over and looked at the simple yet beautiful painting. It was a picture of some men fishing the same pond that you could see out of the office window. Everyone looked so happy.

Jack pointed to the oldest man in the picture and said, "That looks like your Great-Grandpa Willie."

"I think you're right, Jack. Whoa! Look at the man helping the toddler fish. That must be Grandpa Cliff helping my dad! Look how young Grandpa Cliff looks! He still has the same smile, though. Oh man, Dad is wearing a diaper and nothing else! Dad is going to get a kick out of this," I laughed while pointing at the little guy.

"Umm McKay... Who is that other person in the painting?" Jack asked.

I got on my tiptoes to get a better look. The man was standing behind Great-Grandpa Willie. He had a giant toad in his hand and was smiling really big. It looked like he was going to put the frog on Willie's shoulder.

"I don't know, but he looks a lot like Grandpa Cliff. Doesn't he?" I remarked.

Jack grabbed the desk chair and dragged it over to the painting on the wall. He stood on the chair and looked closer at the guy with the toad.

"Hmmm. I am pretty sure this guy is your Grandpa Cliff," Jack said.

"Let me look! There can't be two Grandpa Cliffs in the same painting," I argued.

I pulled Jack off the chair. I hopped on and looked closely at the guy with the toad and then at the guy helping the toddler.

"What do you think, McKay? Do they look the same to you?"

"Holy Moly! Jack, I swear they are the same person. They look identical!" I declared.

"Wait. Does your Grandpa Cliff have an identical twin?"

"No. If my grandpa had a twin, I think I'd know about it," I answered.

Jack and I looked at each other. Our eyes got really big.

"What if he was a twin?" asked Jack.

"Then that would mean Grandpa Cliff has been keeping a giant secret," I declared.

"We should go tell your dad," insisted Jack.

"No, remember at the table how talking about Grandpa Cliff got my dad all worked up? Let's figure this out on our own before we say anything. I mean, it's just a painting. Maybe we are jumping to conclusions here. We need more proof before we make such a big claim," I reasoned.

"Good point. But if it is true... Why would your Grandpa Cliff not want people to know he has a twin? It just doesn't make sense to me," replied Jack.

"Nothing has made sense to me since we moved here, but if anyone can figure out the mystery, it's you and me," I said.

Then Mom's voice called for us from downstairs. We quickly closed the office door and locked it behind us, running downstairs like nothing had happened.

"Hey, Mom. You called?" I asked innocently.

"Your Dad needs your help outside. Do you think you two could help him? He's out by the pond in the backyard," she said.

"Of course. Love you, Mom!" I said as we ran to go help Dad out.

When we got outside, we saw Dad and Dallas raking up leaves. We grabbed a couple of rakes and began to help. As we worked our way around the pond, I couldn't help but think about the painting we had just discovered. I imagined Great-Grandpa Willie enjoying a great day fishing with his family around this exact pond. I laughed a bit, picturing my dad running around with nothing on but a diaper while my Grandpa Cliff tried to catch him a fish. I bet those were happy times for both of them.

I looked over at Dad. He had definitely grown up. It made me sad to think he didn't even remember Great-Grandpa Willie or anything about his childhood home. I thought about how happy I was to be here in Eerie Hollow and how I would be even happier in a few days when deer hunting season started. I walked over to the tree line and looked down at the bare ground. I saw a huge buck track.

"Holy Moly, that is humungous," I whispered to myself.

I honestly had never seen a deer track so big in my whole twelve years on this earth. I followed the tracks a little deeper into the woods. This buck was so heavy that his tracks squished deep into the ground. I was mesmerized by them.

I followed them until they suddenly disappeared. I was so confused. They were so easy to follow, but now they were just gone. It's like the buck vanished into thin air.

I huffed and puffed for a moment in frustration. Then I looked up. My eyes focused on a carving in a big oak tree. In capital letters, right above where the buck tracks ended, was the name CARL....

Chapter 11

Family Secrets

I stood helplessly mesmerized by the name on the tree. My heart started to beat faster and faster.

"Why would Carl's name be carved into this tree? Why would Carl be on Great-Grandpa Willie's property? Could this be the same Carl that went crazy?" I muttered under my breath as a million more questions swirled around my brain.

"Think McKay. Think. What is going on here?"

Then it hit me like a ton of bowling balls. I ran back to the pond but stayed hidden behind some overgrown bushes. I waved my hands silently to get Jack's attention.

Jack looked over at Dad and Dallas. When they weren't looking, he ran over to me.

"What is it?" he asked, with a look on his face that made me feel like he thought I was some kind of weirdo.

I put my finger up to my lips. I grabbed Jack's hand and pulled him inside the house. Together, we ran up to Great-Grandpa Willie's fancy office and opened the door with the large black key.

"What in the world has gotten into you, McKay? What's going on?" Jack whispered loudly.

"I think I figured it out! I know what's going on here. It makes so much sense. It's so obvious now. Carl's name is carved into a tree near our pond!" I said out loud, but not directly to Jack.

"What's obvious? What tree? What are you saying, McKay?" demanded Jack.

"Grandpa Cliff had an identical twin," I said while pacing around the room.

"Something bad happened here that Grandpa Cliff won't talk about," I continued.

"The ghost story," I mumbled.

"The guy telling the ghost story said that he was in school when Carl came crashing in to tell them about the giant buck," I said, starting to grin.

"So? I don't get what you're saying, McKay. Get to the point!" yelled Jack.

"The point is that Carl came into the classroom to tell the teacher that he had seen a ginormous buck! The teacher was Carl's TWIN BROTHER!"

I started laughing. It seemed so obvious all of a sudden.

"Jack, don't you see? Carl had an identical twin brother! Grandpa Cliff had an identical twin brother.

Grandpa Cliff and Crazy Carl are brothers! Identical twin brothers... the painting. Carl is the guy with the toad! That's the big secret. That's what made Grandpa Cliff leave Eerie Hollow. His twin brother became the town's ghost story!"

"Oh wow. Wow. That actually makes sense. No wonder Grandpa Cliff never wanted to come back to Eerie Hollow. His identical twin is The Phantom of Eerie Hollow. I wouldn't want to live here either!" exclaimed Jack.

"That's why Stan was so confused that Dad had never heard of The Phantom of Eerie Hollow. The Phantom is my Dad's uncle!" I explained.

"Stan knew your Dad's uncle was the Phantom even though your dad didn't," said Jack quietly.

"Ok. So, if Stan didn't know that we didn't know about Carl being our relative, why did he give me the key to Great-Grandpa Willie's office? It wasn't so we would see the painting. There has to be something else in here, something that will lead to an adventure. A really exciting adventure. That's what Stan keeps whispering into my ear every time he has a chance," I stated.

Jack and I began to search the room frantically. We looked high and low. We tugged on every book in the library, hoping it would unlock a secret passage, like in the movies. No passage. We looked under the rug to see if there was a trap door. There wasn't. It was exciting and exhausting all at once, but we didn't find anything interesting at all.

"The desk. It's got to be in the desk," I stated.

We pulled out every drawer in the desk but found nothing. All the drawers were completely empty. I fell to the floor in angst. I have to admit that I was being a bit overly dramatic. I layed on the hardwood floor under Great-Grandpa Willie's desk. I put my hands over my eyes, trying to think hard. I stretched my cheeks downward with my hands, pulling my lips into a funny shape.

"Come on, Great-Grandpa Willie. If you want me to find it, you'll have to help me out here," I whispered.

At that moment, I looked up at the underside of Willie's old-fashioned desk and noticed a small hole the size of a finger. So, I did what any reasonable kid would do. I put my finger in the hole. I felt a round wooden button with my fingertip.

"Jack, I think I found something," I said as I slowly pushed the button with my pointer finger.

I felt a click. A small drawer sprung out of the side of the desk! Jack ran over to see what it was. I hopped up off the ground. We both stood over the drawer, looking down into it. In the secret drawer was a leather-bound book titled "Willie's Journal" burnt into the leather.

I carefully lifted the journal out of the hidden drawer. It was old, but there wasn't any dust on the cover. That was odd. I ran my fingers across the burnt letters that spelled out Great-Grandpa's name. A calm feeling came over me as I slowly opened the book to reveal the first page.

"McKay, I don't know if you should be reading someone's journal," Jack cautiously stated.

"I don't know how to describe it, but I feel like it was written for me to read. Besides, journals of dead people are meant to be read. That's why people write in them," I remarked quietly.

I thumbed through the hundreds of pages of the journal. Beautiful, cursive handwriting filled them. There were so many pages that I didn't know where to start. It would take forever to read it. I thought for a second, trying to figure out what it was that Great-Grandpa Willie wanted me to read.

"It has to be something to do with his son Carl going crazy. When did that happen?" I asked Jack.

We both scrunched our faces, wondering what year the ghost story started.

"The guy with the bushy mustache just said many, many moons ago when he was telling the ghost story," remembered Jack.

"That's not helpful at all. We need a date that is a little more concrete," I replied.

I looked around the room for ideas or clues. My eyes fell on the painting of the pond. I looked at my diaper-clad father. An idea popped into my head!

"Jack, in the painting, my dad is a toddler, and I know Grandpa Cliff left Eerie Hollow when Dad was barely walking. Does the painting have a date on it by chance?" I asked.

Jack jumped out of his seat and pulled the chair back to the painting. He got up and looked in the bottom corner next to the frame.

"You're a genius, McKay. There is a date that says 1934 under a signature that says... You're not going to believe this. It was right in front of our eyes the whole time. The signature says, Carl!" Jack boomed.

"Duh, Carl was an artist! The storyteller said that Carl shared his time between his love of painting and cheering up the town's kids," I said, shaking my head.

"All the paintings in this house are probably his. If this painting was painted in 1934, then it's likely that Carl went crazy in the fall of that same year since he went nutso during hunting season," Jack reasoned.

I turned the pages of the journal until I reached October 1934. I saw a string of entries mentioning Carl.

Chapter 12

Willie's Journal

October 1, 1934

Upon his return home this evening, my son, Carl, was in a splendid mood. He shared with me that he would harvest the largest buck he says he's ever seen. Whatever the results of this hunting might be, Carl's joy is all I care for.

He began a new painting endeavor. I believe it helps show how he feels and thinks about the beauty of these creatures. His gift is evident, and he concentrates intensely, even chewing on his paintbrush.

October 6, 1934

Carl's demeanor is usually more light and playful than it has been as of late. He doesn't seem to smile as easily. Here at our place, around eight o'clock in the morning, he told me this new buck, his obsession, has glowing white eyes—such nonsense.

When he is here at the house, he seems uneasy about his present circumstance. When I happened upon him while painting, he barely glanced at me. All his time seems consumed with this "Phantom Buck," as he calls it.

October 13, 1934

Tonight, as I drove home from my four-days-long business trip, my thoughts turned to my son Carl. I wanted to see how he was reacting to the present situation. Upon my return home, I discovered that he seemed to be losing his mind about it all. His apparel is unchanged from day to day. His appearance is unbecoming of a son of mine.

I also noticed that he hung his new masterpiece at the top of the grand staircase. It is a remarkable painting, but I fear it was born of an unhealthy obsession.

October 15, 1934

Today, Cliff and Carl argued loudly. Over what, I do not know. However, tonight, by way of explanation, Cliff discussed his concern for his brother's well-being after Carl stormed out of the house.

Cliff reports Carl has named his target buck "The Phantom of Eerie Hollow" due to the animal's glowing eyes and ability to disappear into thin air.

Although I believe my boys should settle their dispute between them, I shared my belief that Carl's excellent hunting skills would prevail. Once Carl harvests this nuisance, all will be well.

November 1, 1934

A most concerning new turn, Carl has been missing for several days. However, his favorite foods keep disappearing from the kitchen, leading me to believe he remains close by. An entire jar of pickled eggs has gone missing, as well as bottles of milk from the ice box.

Puzzling out his whereabouts is a long, discouraging task. Where is my son hiding?

November 2, 1934

I was much surprised this morning when I found Carl rummaging and packing supplies. My elation in seeing him gave way to dismay as he refused to disclose his whereabouts these last days. Not only that, but said that he would never tell me and that I would never know, which seems to me a combative stance.

His demeanor is someone entirely different than who I know my son to be. His mind has fallen into illness and obsession. I asked many questions and tried to discuss his actions, but he refused. He left in the same filthy clothing he has been wearing for weeks. I'm confused further because he left wearing only his red socks but no boots.

November 15, 1934

Carl returned to the house today looking white as a ghost and completely unwell. He has not been sleeping; he says he lies awake all of the night. His joints are aching as well. According to Carl, this is all happening because of his

Phantom of Eerie Hollow. He is so consumed that I cannot help but believe him. He refuses help of any kind, including the doctor in town.

November 22, 1934

Carl has disappeared in the mansion once more; he's been gone for days despite my constant searching. He screams and howls at night; I can hear the faint sounds of his tortured mind as I sleep in my bed chambers.

Cliff has made his position known; he wants to stop Carl from his hunting of the Phantom Buck, but I believe Carl will be victorious yet.

November 29, 1934

Carl appeared once more on this day of Thanksgiving. However, there was not much to be thankful for in his reappearance. His odor was foul, as he had not bathed in weeks. He has not changed his clothing since this obsession began. Trembling hands held his hunting rifle, giving proof that he was not well.

To my dismay, he was preparing to enter the woods once more to bring an end to his Phantom. He claims to have mapped the entire forest and knows where to bag his buck. On a separate note, he claimed to have extreme stomach pain, to which I replied that he should visit a doctor. He would not listen to reason.

November 30, 1934

I heard Carl on the porch this evening rocking in his chair. He sang some nonsense song while playing his harmonica. The degenerate Creedy brothers arrived at the porch around nine o'clock and began to bully him regarding the Phantom. I hurried downstairs to chase them off, but I arrived too late.

In fatherly horror, I watched as Carl marched silently down Main Street. I hurried after him to no avail. He jumped on the stage at the festival, and slammed his lantern down causing the stage to catch on fire. He vowed a curse upon the town that terrified me as a father. He vowed that he would never return without the Phantom in his arms, and if he never returned, he would haunt the town.

Cliff tried to stop him from going into the woods, but Carl would not be swayed. I told Cliff to let his brother go. Carl ran into the woods. Cliff shared his anger with me for allowing Carl to go.

December 15th 1934

A blizzard hit the town hard in the night. This morning, around seven o'clock, I opened the front doors to find that it had snowed two feet. It's been two weeks since Carl vowed never to return without his Phantom. I am losing hope. I know he was not well in body or mind. Cliff searches the woods daily, trying to find his lost brother. He blames me for letting Carl enter the woods that dreadful night. I fear that I may lose both of my sons in this tragedy.

December 25th 1934

Today is Christmas and yet I celebrated it alone. This mansion is now very empty and hollow. Cliff took his son and left forever. He blames me for losing his brother Carl. We can only assume that Carl is now dead. The townspeople on the other hand are now calling Carl "The Phantom of Eerie Hollow". People claim to hear his harmonica in the woods, and that he is haunting the town. My heart is broken. I don't understand.

I looked over at Jack. His light blue eyes were welling up a little bit with tears. Mine were, too. I could barely see the journal because my eyes were so watery.

What an incredibly sad story. I felt bad for each of them, but my heart hurt so badly for Great-Grandpa Willie. His whole life got turned upside down. He was so happy and had family surrounding him, but everyone left him alone in this mansion.

I felt terrible for Grandpa Cliff. What a horrible thing to have happened to your twin. From what I've been told, twins are super connected to each other. It must have felt like he lost a big part of himself when Carl disappeared forever. I understood why he never wanted to talk about this place. He was probably really upset with Dad for moving us to Eerie Hollow.

I also felt awful for Carl. His life was turned upside down because of this Phantom Buck. I just can't believe that an animal could have this kind of effect on someone. He literally went out of his mind. He was a real person with real feelings. He wasn't just a ghost story.

I turned the ancient pages of the journal and noticed that mentions of Carl and Cliff became rare. I turned to the last entry and began to read. My heart almost beat out of my chest at what he wrote....

Chapter 13

Final Request

August 31, 1969

McKay, my Great-Grandson, you are a clever boy for having found my journal. I'm proud of you for discovering the secret to my desk. I hope that problem-solving quality leads you to fulfill my final request: Bring Carl home.

Somewhere in this mansion is a secret room that I could never find. Carl hid from us for weeks at a time in this secret place. Find that room. Learn what he was up to. Then, find Carl. Don't do it for me. Do it for your Grandpa Cliff. Give Cliff the closure that he needs, that I could never give to him. Find his twin. You are the ONE to do it.

With Love,

Great-Grandpa Willie

I looked over at Jack with big eyes.

"He wrote to me directly. I never even knew Great-Grandpa Willie. Why does he think I can find Carl's secret hiding place and find Carl in the deep, dark, haunted woods when they never could?" I asked sincerely.

"McKay, I have never met anyone as good at figuring out mysteries as you. I mean, you figured out the whole Cliff and Carl twin thing on your own. With a little bit of my help, I'm sure you can find Carl's hiding place," Jack explained.

"Oh man, this has gotten heavy. Let's go outside and think. I want to show you Carl's name carved in the tree," I shared.

We went outside. Dad and Dallas had finished raking the leaves, but they were nowhere to be found. The pond really looked beautiful. It was a clear day, and the blue autumn sky reflected in the water. I decided that nature really is something to stop and appreciate. Jack and I walked over to the edge of the pond. I picked up a flat, round rock and tossed it at the perfect angle to skip it. I counted each skip the rock made as it traveled halfway across the pond.

"Seven skips!" I bragged to Jack.

Jack grabbed a flat rock and did the same, except his rock went further than mine and skipped nine times. Jack gave me a cocky wink.

Not to be outdone, I looked around for the perfect skipping stone and saw one in the water at the very edge of the pond. I looked over and saw that Jack saw it, too. We both raced to be the first to grab it. I reached my hand into the water. Suddenly, I felt a mammoth-sized hand on my back.

Before I realized what was happening, I was flying face-first into the water! I felt the cold pond water go up my nose as my body went under. I scrambled to get my head above the water to breathe. When I finally broke the water's surface, I looked around to find the fiend that pushed me.

The first face I saw was Uncle Dallas! He was belly laughing so hard. My loving uncle had pushed me into the pond! I looked to my side and saw that Jack had been pushed in, too. We looked at each other and nodded. We didn't have to say a word. We knew what we needed to do. We swam to the shore. Water splashed everywhere as we pulled ourselves out of the pond. We were soaking wet and wanted more than anything to return the wet favor to Uncle Dallas. We closed in on him. He had his eyes shut because he was laughing so hard.

We each grabbed a hand of Dallas' to try and pull him into the water. We pulled and tugged, but he didn't move an inch. In fact, in a humiliating fashion, he picked each of us up off the ground, leaving our wet feet dangling in the air. Jack in Dallas' right hand and me in his left. We had been bested again by this childish Viking man that we loved so much.

With his feet still off the ground dangling like a wind chime, Jack vowed in a powerful voice, "We will get you back, Dad! I don't know when, but we will get you!"

"Oh, I'm super worried about that," Dallas joked with a look on his face as if he knew there was nothing we could do to fulfill that vow.

Dallas set us down on our feet. Jack and I gave him a big wet hug to ensure he got a little wet from pushing us into the pond. Then we all decided to go inside to warm up and change our clothes. The tree with Carl's name on it would have to wait.

We ran to our room and got into some dry clothes. Then we decided we might as well start looking for the secret room that Carl hid in while he was at home. Honestly, we didn't even know where to start. The mansion was huge. I couldn't figure out how we could find a secret room that Great-Grandpa Willie couldn't find after all these years. He knew every inch of the mansion he had built for his family.

We decided to start from the bottom and work our way up. We checked the basement and found a ton of spiders. Jack even found a Black Widow.

"Black Widows make my skin crawl," admitted Jack.

He took off his shoes and clapped them together where the spider was hanging in her web. The Black Widow exploded. It was gross, but it had to be done. We couldn't leave that killing machine alive to get us in our sleep someday.

We searched every corner of the basement without any luck. We went to the first floor and opened every door we could find. There were a lot of doors, but none seemed to be a good hiding place. I walked past the fireplace where Great-Grandpa Willie's ashes sat quietly on the mantel. I briefly looked at the urn and thought the fireplace might have something hidden in it. So, I climbed inside where the fire would usually be and looked up. Nope. Nothing but a chimney that needed to be cleaned. I pushed on every brick to see if any of them were loose. None were.

We went to the second floor and did a deep search. Great-Grandpa Willie's office was the only interesting room we found up there. We didn't go into the master bedroom, though. There was no way Carl made his secret hideout in his dad's room, and there was no way I was going to get caught snooping in there by my mom. She would ground me for a week! So, we went up to the creepiest attic I had ever seen.

The attic was even more spooky than the basement. There weren't any lights up there, so we had to use our flashlights to see anything. There were boxes filled with paintings from Carl's childhood. He definitely had a natural gift. I looked at one picture with "Carl, Second Grade" written on the back. It was a painting of a beautiful sunset with two boys sitting on a rock together, watching the sun go to sleep. I looked at the boys and tried to imagine Carl and Grandpa Cliff spending time together. I bet you they were genuinely inseparable as kids.

While I was looking at the painting, Jack called me over.

"McKay, I pulled this rug to the side and found this!" he exclaimed excitedly.

I looked down at where he was pointing and saw what looked like a trap door!

"Jack! Nice work! Do you think this could be it?" I asked loudly.

"There's only one way to find out," he said as he slipped his fingers into a crack in the floorboards.

He slowly opened the trap door. I shined my light into the dark opening. The beam of my flashlight lit up the compartment the same way that our eyes lit up with excitement.

Chapter 14

Box of Tricks

The trap door wasn't the entry to Carl's hideout, but it was the hiding place for Carl's box of tricks and pranks! Oh man, it was like Christmas for me! Jack and I went through the box and got more excited with each item.

The first thing we saw was hundreds of firecrackers. I couldn't wait to light them up! There was also a Whoopee Cushion, smoke bombs, sleeping pills, fake spiders, stink bombs, fake .270 rifle cartridges (I had no idea what they did), and a fake rattlesnake that rattled on its own. The snake had a spring-loaded mechanism that made it so it could strike at a poor, unsuspecting soul! The box also had more practical things, like glue, a lighter, and metal tacks.

Talk about a treasure! I was absolutely sure that Carl and I would have gotten along great. I wished I could have met him. Jack seemed to be having just as much fun as I was going through the box of tricks. That's when Jack's "I have an idea" face lit up.

"So, you know how we are trying to find Carl's hiding place?" he asked.

"Of course," I responded, knowing that something exciting would come out of Jack's mouth at any moment.

"What if we were to channel our inner Carl and play a prank on my dad? He totally deserves to get scared out of his shorts for pushing us into the pond, right?" he said deviously.

"Yes! I love it. Which trick should we do?" I asked.

"Well, I'm trying to decide between the fake rattlesnake and the firecrackers," he quipped.

"What if we put the firecrackers in a pot at the top of the stairs? Then, when we hear Dallas come out of his bedroom and walk our way, we light them and hide," I schemed.

"Perfect. It's almost time for dinner, right? My dad said he was going to take a nap before we ate. We could catch him on his way down to eat," Jack said.

"I love it!" I exclaimed.

So, we grabbed a few dozen firecrackers or so. Then we put the prank box back where we found it under the trap door. We ran downstairs and peeked into the kitchen. Mom was making spaghetti. It smelled so good. My mom had some serious spaghetti-making skills. She always used deer meat from the freezer.

Knowing that it had deer in it made me like it even more.

"Jack, I'll create a small diversion to get my mom's attention. You grab a pot when she's not looking. Deal?" I whispered.

He gave me a thumbs-up. I walked over to my mom. I had to think quickly of a way to get her attention on me and not on Jack grabbing a pot. I knew exactly what to do. I tapped Mom on the shoulder, and when she turned around, I gave her a giant hug. I squished her head into my neck as I hugged her tightly. I watched over her shoulder as Jack quickly opened the cabinet and grabbed a big, red pot. He did it in absolute silence, and as soon as he made his escape, I ended the hug with Mom. She looked at me suspiciously.

"McKay, what are you up to?" she asked with curious eyes.

"Nothing, Mom. Can't a son hug his all-time favorite mom whenever he feels like it?" I said with a cheesy smile.

"He can, but it would be nice if he did it without ulterior motives," she replied.

She was seriously so good at knowing when I was up to no good!

"Umm, love you! Bye!" I hollered as I ran out of the kitchen.

I turned the corner and saw Jack. He was laughing at me.

"Your mom knows you too well," he said through his laughter.

"It's true, but it worked. Didn't it?" I said as I grabbed the pot out of Jack's hands.

We ran up the stairs and set the pot down a few feet in front of the big painting of the giant buck.

"Umm, maybe that's too close to the painting. I don't want to ruin Carl's masterpiece," I explained as I moved the pot further towards the edge of the hallway.

I reached into my pocket and grabbed the lighter. I flicked it several times to ensure it still worked after a lifetime of not being used. Sure enough, it did.

Just then, Mom yelled from the kitchen, "Dinner is ready! Come get it while it's hot!"

Uncle Dallas loved to eat more than anything and was always the first to the table. Dallas opened his door the moment Mom yelled. We heard footsteps coming in our direction. I lit the firecrackers, and we retreated down a few stairs and ducked to try and hide. Just as Uncle Dallas came around the corner of the hallway, the firecrackers started to explode! We had timed it perfectly.

Uncle Dallas fell to the ground like he was getting ambushed. Once he hit the floor, he covered his head with his massive arms.

But the best part was when he screamed, "Holy tarnation, we're under attack. Golly gosh darn it to heck, we're all going to die. Take cover. Ahhhhh!"

Then, when the firecrackers stopped exploding, he slowly lifted his head over his bulging arms. That's when we jumped up from the stairs and began to point and laugh.

"Uncle Dallas, we got you so good! I've never seen you so scared in my life," I hollered.

I held my belly to laugh like he did after throwing us in the pond.

"Do you need to change your pants, Dad? I mean, if you peed a little, it would be totally understandable," laughed Jack.

Dallas didn't get mad at all. In fact, a smile broke across his face. I think we impressed him with our prank. He even started to laugh as he pointed at the firecracker pot.

"Oh boy, that was a good one, kids! I can't believe you actually got me. I was scared to death," he admitted.

I looked at the pot. It was still smoking from the explosion that it endured. That's when I noticed something a bit odd. The smoke wasn't rising straight up. It was getting sucked behind the eerie buck painting.

"What in the world is going on up there!" Mom yelled at the top of her lungs.

I looked down the stairs and saw Mom staring at us with violent eyes. Dallas may have thought our little prank was funny, but my mom definitely did not!

"Umm, we just played a prank on Dallas. We were getting him back for pushing us into the pond," I tried to explain.

Mom stomped up the stairs. When she reached the top, she looked down and saw her favorite red pot filled with firecracker debris.

"You lit firecrackers in the house? What were you thinking? That's a huge fire hazard and not safe at all! You put us and this house in danger! Firecrackers are no joke! Go to your room now! Both of you!" she yelled at the top of her lungs.

While we ran past her to go to our room, she hollered, "I knew your hug wasn't sincere! You were just keeping my eyes off of your deviant cousin while he snatched my pot! No dinner for either of you tonight!"

We opened the door to our room. My heart sank for a second as I realized I had used a hug to deceive my mom. I probably should not have done that. I looked over at Jack, and he looked a little remorseful as well, but that only lasted for a second before we both started laughing our heads off.

"Holy moly! Did you see your dad's face when the firecrackers went off? I exclaimed, laughing so hard.

"I have never seen my Dad so scared in my life, and I've seen him chase a grizzly out of our campsite in Alaska!" he acknowledged.

I laughed some more, and then I remembered the smoke from the firecrackers. An idea popped into my head.

"Jack, I think I know where Carl was hiding...."

Chapter 15

The Theory

We hung out in our room until dinner was over. I paced across my bedroom floor as I tried to put clues together.

"Jack, in the journal, remember how Great Grandpa Willie said that Carl started a giant painting after he came home from seeing the Phantom Buck for the first time?" I asked.

"Ya, I do. What painting do you think it was? There are paintings of bucks all over this house," Jack said.

"At the top of the stairs. That is The Phantom of Eerie Hollow. It has to be. It's ginormous, has white eyes, and has a creepy mist covering some of its body," I reminded him.

"Ok, so what if it is?" asked Jack.

"The smoke from the firecracker was going behind that painting. There has to be an opening back there. Smoke doesn't flow into a solid wall. Also, remember how Willie said he went on a four-day-long work trip while Carl was going looney? I bet you that is when Carl built the room and then covered it with the new painting," I explained.

"I mean, I guess that makes sense. But it for sure doesn't prove anything. It's a good theory at best," Jack challenged.

"Well, the only way to determine if I'm right is to check behind the painting. Easy peasy lemon squeezy," I replied.

We waited until it was past bedtime. There was no way I wanted to run into Mom again. Once we decided the coast was clear, we grabbed our flashlights and snuck out of our bedroom. All the lights were off, a sure sign that Mom had made her way to bed. We snuck up the stairs and looked at the painting. I could have sworn that the eyes of the Phantom Buck followed me up the stairs. It was like the buck was looking into my soul.

When we got to the painting, I quietly put my fingers behind the solid silver frame. There was a slight crack between the painting and the wall, where I saw the smoke disappear. I pulled on the frame, expecting to move the painting and reveal a room, but the painting didn't budge.

"Jack, help me pull on the painting. It's stuck," I whispered.

He put his fingers behind the left side of the frame, and I pulled on the right side. We grunted quietly as we pulled with all our combined strength, but the painting didn't move.

"Well, it was a good idea, McKay, but I think you were wrong. This painting isn't moving."

I sat down crosslegged in front of the masterful painting and stared at it. I looked the buck in the eyes. The whiteness of his eyes was super intense. Something felt strange about that.

"Jack, have you ever seen a deer with white eyes? I thought deer's eyes were always black," I said.

"Ya, McKay, you're right. A normal buck has dark eyes. I wonder why this buck had white eyes. It makes sense that Carl thought it was a phantom," he said.

"I can see why Carl was obsessed with this buck. Look at that rack. He has antlers for days! The double drop tines are super unique, too. No way you could confuse this buck with any other," I admitted.

I looked at the painting a little longer. I couldn't let go of the idea that this had to be the entrance to Carl's lair.

"In the journal, didn't Willie say that when he was in his bedroom, he could hear Carl screaming?" inquired Jack.

"You're right. He definitely said that. The master bedroom is the closest room to this painting. Jack, we are missing something. This has to be it. Maybe there is a secret lever or something that opens it. You know, just like the finger hole in Willie's desk," I whispered hopefully.

Jack nodded, and we started to search for anything that could be a lever. We looked up at the two buck mounts on either side of the painting.

"Maybe one of the tines of the antlers is a lever, or an eyeball is a button?" I stated.

I went straight to work on the buck mount on the right of the painting, and Jack worked on the one on the left. I tugged on its ears. I poked the mount's eyes. I grabbed each antler and pulled. I twisted the whole mount on the wall like a steering wheel, and nothing happened. I started to lose hope. We were never going to find it.

"Ummm... McKay... Look..."

I looked over at my cousin. I watched his fingers closely as he twisted his buck mount's right eye guard to the left. He kept twisting. My jaw dropped to the floor....

Chapter 16

Tiny Key

"Jack! What did you find?" I whisper shouted.

"The whole eye guard unscrewed from the mount, and it's hollow! The smallest key I have ever seen is inside the antler!" Jack shouted a little too loud.

Suddenly, the door to my parent's room opened. Jack and I were horror-struck. If that was Mom, we were dead meat. I learned a long time ago not to get her upset twice on the same day!

We panicked and ran down the stairs, passing the giant bronze hunter statue. We turned the corner and ran to our room. We opened the door, ran inside, and then shut the door quickly but quietly behind us. We turned off the light and jumped into our separate beds.

We waited patiently, hoping and praying Mom would not come into our room. Suddenly, we heard a gentle tapping at the door. Our stomachs dropped, giving each of us a sick feeling deep inside.

"Boys, are you in there?" my dad inquired.

My heart slowed down a bit when I heard Dad's voice instead of Mom's.

"Ya, Dad, we're in bed. Come on in," I called out.

Dad opened the door and turned on the light. Jack and I both pretended that the light was hurting our eyes since we had been innocently sleeping in the dark for hours now.

"Hey, guys. Sorry for waking you. Something woke me up, and I couldn't go back to sleep," Dad claimed.

I looked over at Jack and saw him breathe out a sigh of relief.

"I just wanted to apologize for how snappy I was earlier when you asked questions about your Grandpa Cliff," he admitted.

"Oh, Dad. No worries. I know that Grandpa Cliff has some strong feelings about this place," I said.

I was careful not to mention anything we had discovered over the past twenty-four hours.

"I just don't understand it, son. Eerie Hollow has been wonderful so far. This house is amazing. The property is beautiful. I can't seem to figure out why Grandpa Cliff hates this place so much. I kind of wish he had never left, and I could have grown up here," he shared.

"I get it, Dad. I wish you could have grown up here, too! I'm sorry he is being so difficult. Maybe, with time, we will figure out what is going on and a way to make things better," I said, sounding pretty wise if you asked me.

"I hope so. Anyway, sorry to bother you. Go back to sleep, and I'll see you in the morning."

"Hey, Dad? Deer season starts the day after tomorrow. Would it be alright if Jack and I go out hunting, just the two of us? We will be careful, we promise," I asked in the kindest, most hopeful voice.

"I'll have to talk to your mom about that one. You two sure got her upset today. Maybe a sincere apology might help a bit before we get her feelings on you guys hunting alone," he advised.

"Smart thinking. Night, Dad."

Dad turned off the light and shut the door. He made his way back up the stairs. I hopped out of bed and turned on the light.

"Show me the key! Show me the key!" I begged excitedly.

Jack pulled the hollow eye guard out of his pocket and brought it to me. I carefully took the little black key out of the antler. It was super tiny. I'd say it was probably no more than an inch long. The end of the key was jagged. It looked homemade. I rolled the tiny key between my fingers. I thought about the potential places the key could go.

"Let's see if we can find a keyhole to stick this into. It has to open up the painting somehow," I said as I walked towards the door.

"McKay, you want to go out there again tonight? Are you crazy? If your mom catches us out there, I really doubt she will let us go hunting alone," he reasoned.

"Fine. You're right. It's not worth getting caught over. We will just have to check in the morning when the grownups are distracted with something else," I said as I got back into bed.

Chapter 17

Carl's Tree

That night, I slept so well. My mind definitely needed a break from all the excitement of the past couple of days. I wish I could say the same thing for Jack. He woke up in the middle of the night in a cold sweat. He screamed something about a giant grizzly, then went back to sleep.

In the morning, I asked him about it, and he denied it ever happened. I think he was kind of embarrassed or too proud to admit that he was scared of something. He got up, opened the door, and walked out of the room.

I followed him to the dining room, where we had breakfast with the family. While we ate, Jack and I sincerely apologized to my mom. I told her that I'd never hug her again for trouble-making purposes. Dallas chimed in and took some blame for the incident since we were just getting him back for pushing us into the pond.

Then, without being asked, we washed Mom's favorite pot. Luckily, the firecrackers didn't do any permanent damage. We did the rest of the dishes while we were at it. It kind of felt good to do something nice for once.

After breakfast, the adults decided that they were going to go to town to do some shopping. They asked if we wanted to go, but we kindly refused. Honestly, I would rather get a tooth pulled at the dentist than go shopping with my parents. It's seriously the most boring thing in the world.

I couldn't wait for them to leave. Jack and I had big plans. We had mysteries to solve. I looked over at Jack. I was thankful that I had Jack here with me. This mansion would be a bit lonely if I were the only kid here. Plus, solving a mystery is always more fun when you have an accomplice.

My parents waved goodbye and shut the front door. Jack and I ran up the stairs past the bronze statue of the giant hunter and stood on the landing. We stared at the painting of The Phantom of Eerie Hollow. There had to be a tiny keyhole somewhere. We carefully inspected the silver frame, looking for a place to put the key, but we found nothing. We searched the entire wall where the painting hung. Nothing. I swear we searched for hours looking for a keyhole, but there just wasn't one to be found.

"Why would there be a hidden key in a hollowed-out antler if there was no keyhole to put it into?" I asked myself out loud.

"No clue. But I'm ready for a break. Want to show me Carl's name carved into the tree?" asked Jack.

"Sure. I could use a break, too. Let's go check it out."

We ran down the stairs and out the front door. The weather was a bit chilly. It definitely felt like deer season.

"This cooler weather should get those deer moving. I can't wait to go hunting tomorrow. Do you think our parents will let you and I go alone?" I asked.

"I'm hopeful. They are super busy getting everything done with the mansion. I don't think they have the time to take us out themselves," said Jack.

We walked past the pond and went into the woods. I found the giant buck track that led me to the tree last time and followed it. When we got to the tree, I showed Jack how the tracks had disappeared entirely. Then I showed him the carving in the tree. He reached up and ran his finger over every letter of Carl's name.

"You know, it's kind of interesting how a few weeks ago, neither of us had ever heard of Carl, and now he is part of almost every conversation," Jack shared.

Jack kneeled down over the last giant buck track. While he was inspecting the track, I looked around. We weren't too far away from the house. It was amazing that such an enormous deer would be this close to the mansion. I looked around from where I stood. The terrain dipped down into a hollow. Jack and I mindlessly walked down the hill for a few seconds. Most of the leaves had fallen now, and the ground crunched with every step we took.

I stopped and looked back at the tree with Carl's name in it. That's when everything changed forever....

Chapter 18

Phantom Buck

He couldn't have been over fifty yards from me. He was looking straight at me. His gaze was penetrating. His eyes were white. I blinked over and over again to make sure I was really seeing what I thought I saw. Standing broadside next to Carl's tree was the Phantom Buck from Carl's painting. I knew that was impossible, but this buck looked exactly like the buck in Carl's masterpiece! The antlers were identical all the way down to the double drop tines. The drop tine on his right antler even had the same lobster claw tine as the painting. But it was his white eyes that convinced me it had to be the same buck.

My heart started to pound hard. I began to freak out on the inside. I didn't know what to do. I broke my gaze at the buck and looked for Jack. I needed him to see it, too. I needed him to see the white eyes and the lobster-claw drop tine. I needed to know I wasn't going crazy, but Jack was nowhere to be seen.

I looked back to the place where the buck had been standing proudly, but he was gone. He had disappeared without a sound. I didn't hear any crunching leaves or snapping branches. Silence. Silence was the only thing I heard. I ran back to the place where the buck had stood. I found a new set of tracks sunk deep into the soft soil. I got down on my knees and looked to see which direction he had gone, but there were no other tracks in the bare dirt. Just four hoof prints standing next to Carl's tree. It's like he vanished into thin air.

"Jack! Jack! Jack! Get up here!" I yelled at the top of my lungs.

Jack heard me and ran to where I was standing. I held my mouth open in complete shock.

"What's going on, McKay? You look like you've seen a ghost," stated Jack.

"I think I might have," I mumbled, shaking my head in disbelief.

"Umm, would you like to explain what you mean by that?" asked Jack.

"I saw him. I really saw him..."

"You saw who?"

"I saw The Phantom of Eerie Hollow. He was standing right here. He uh... he uh... vanished," I stuttered.

I pointed at the ground and showed Jack the four deep tracks. He put his hand in them.

"These are the same tracks you showed me before. Are you alright? Wait, what do you mean you saw The Phantom of Eerie Hollow? It can't be the same buck that Carl was chasing thirty-something years ago. Deer don't live that long. Do they?" Jack asked, with a tinge of fear in his voice.

"You're right. Deer don't live that long, Jack. But his antlers were exactly the same as the buck in the painting. I promise you. It was that buck," I gulped.

Then I continued, "His eyes were white. When he looked at me, it felt like he was piercing my soul. It was overwhelming."

We stood there in silence for a few more minutes. I didn't know how to interpret the situation I found myself in. I had seen the Phantom Buck. I knew I had. My heart felt full. I began to sweat. I felt weak in my knees. This all couldn't be a coincidence. Everything that I had learned up to this point, and on top of that, actually seeing the Phantom. It all felt like it had to be destiny.

We made our way back to the mansion. We opened the large, eight-foot tall, oak front doors and entered the fancy, marble-tiled entryway. I looked over at the mantle above the fireplace where Great-Grandpa Willie's ashes rested, and his giant self-portrait hung. I knew he needed me to figure this out. My mind was racing a hundred miles an hour. I paced as I pondered the events of the day, and that's when I tripped over my own feet and fell face-first onto the tile floor.

I hit my head on the hard marble tile. I groaned as I reached my hand to my forehead to see if I was bleeding. Luckily, I wasn't, but man, did that hurt! While laying face first on the cool tile, my gaze turned towards the grand staircase. My eyes followed the stairs up to the second floor, where Carl's masterpiece hung proudly. I shook my head as I looked at the Phantom Buck in the painting. He looked exactly like the buck I saw next to Carl's tree.

I sighed out loud. It just didn't make sense to me. Not even a little bit. I broke my gaze from the painting and looked at the giant bronze hunter. From where I lay on the floor, I could see straight down the barrel of his old-fashioned muzzleloader. When we first moved into the mansion, I noticed that the hunter was pointing his muzzleloader at the painting. But now, lying on the ground, looking down the barrel, I noticed something very, very strange.

"Jack, the giant bronze hunter isn't aiming at the Phantom Buck," I remarked carefully.

"That is weird. What is he aiming at?" asked Jack.

"He's aiming at the rocks behind the buck. Why would Carl hang the painting in a place where the hunter wasn't aiming at the Phantom Buck? That seems super strange to me," I said as a flash of brilliance hit my mind.

"Jack, go upstairs and check the rocks for a keyhole!" I shouted excitedly.

Jack ran up the stairs and got on his tiptoes. He carefully ran his fingers across the rocks. I looked down the barrel, and when his finger hit the spot the hunter was aiming at, I yelled, "Stop! Right there! Is there a hole? Please tell me there is a keyhole!" I hollered, hopefully.

"McKay, you are a genius! There is a hole. Let me see if the key fits," he said.

I got on my feet and ran up the stairs. There was no way I was going to let Jack open the secret pathway without me! When I got up to the painting, Jack looked at me. I nodded with a grin on my face. He slowly turned the key....

Chapter 19

Carl's Lair

Jack turned the key to the left until we heard a clicking sound. The painting swung open effortlessly. We both smiled really big. We had found Carl's secret lair! Great-Grandpa Willie would have been so proud of us! Oh, I wished he was here to see this. He searched for thirty-five years without finding it. Poor guy just needed a couple of twelve-year-olds to help!

We looked into the pitch-black room. We couldn't see anything. Jack and I decided to be brave and stepped into the darkness.

As we walked in, our legs got caught on something. Neither of us fell to the floor, but we heard a whirring sound, and almost immediately, we felt a heavy net cover our whole bodies. There were bells attached to the net, and they jingled as we struggled to get out of the booby trap! The entire house must have been filled with the sound of bells. Good thing Mom and Dad weren't home!

Jack and I tried to escape the room to see how we had been trapped. We struggled with the weight of the net, but finally, we fell out of the hidden lair onto the floor in front of the painting.

My heart leaped out of my chest. I saw Black Widow spiders all over the net! They were everywhere!

"Ahhhhhh! Jack, get them off of me! Get them off of me," I shrieked.

But I wasn't the only one screaming! Jack was now screaming, too. He was slapping the net with his hands, trying to knock the lady assassins away!

"Black Widows are on me! I'm going to die! Help! Help! Help!" Jack cried out loud.

We struggled until we found the opening at the bottom of the net and shimmied ourselves out of its grasp. The net rested on the ground in silence. The loud bells stopped ringing, but my ears continued to ring almost as loud as my heart was pounding.

I focused on the spiders. I noticed that none of them were actually moving... I reached out and picked one up. It was plastic. I shook my head side to side as a big grin broke out across my face. I didn't know whether I should hate Carl for setting this booby trap or if I should stand up and applaud with complete admiration.

Jack let out a sigh of relief when he realized that the Black Widows were fake. He took a couple of big, deep breaths. Then he started laughing out loud.

"OK, this Carl guy was awesome! That was quite the trap. I'm actually really glad your Great-Grandpa Willie never found Carl's lair. He would have died way earlier from a heart attack!" claimed Jack.

We both laid on the floor for a few minutes as the adrenaline worked its way through our bodies. Then we stood up together and decided that we should go get our flashlights. We ran downstairs, got them, and came back to the lair. We shined our lights at the entry and saw that we had tripped on a fishing line. The fishing line ran about six inches from the floor, up the wall, and up to the ceiling. A dangling metal pin was attached to the fishing line. I looked above the pin and saw it had been pulled out of a mechanism that held the net up. When the pin got yanked out of the mechanism, the net fell.

"Brilliant. Just brilliant," I declared in awe.

"Look for a light switch. There's no way Carl hid in here for weeks at a time without light," suggested Jack.

I shined my light around the room and saw a pull string a few feet in front of my eyes hanging from the ceiling. I pulled the string. Christmas lights that were carefully hung on the ceiling all turned on at once. It was beautiful. There were hundreds of little lights. We marveled at the beauty of the lights for a moment. Something seemed very familiar about them. I tilted my head and tried to think what they reminded me of... Stars... They looked like stars in the night sky. I looked closer and saw The Big Dipper perfectly recreated with the Christmas lights. I smiled. He had charted the stars in the sky! I pointed at a constellation.

"Look, Jack, it's Orion," I stated, very pleased with myself.

"What are you talking about? Orion, who?"Jack replied.

"Orion, The Hunter, is right there. The lights are stars. Look, over there is The Big Dipper," I said while pointing.

"Whoa, you're right! Amazing! It's beautiful," admitted Jack.

As I looked at the lights, I noticed one light was brighter than the others. It was the star at the end of the handle of the Little Dipper, which meant that it was the North Star.

"This must have taken weeks to put up and get right. The lights exactly match the stars in the night sky.

I looked over at Jack. He found an actual light switch. He flipped it on. The whole lair lit up. We both gasped as we saw the workings of a mad genius.

Chapter 20

Diorama

Carl had indeed gone crazy. That was all I could think of as I looked at the room. There was no other explanation. Hundreds of pairs of white eyes had been painted on the walls and the ceiling. I had to assume that they were the white eyes of The Phantom of Eerie Hollow. I had seen them myself earlier that day and had felt them look deep into my soul. They must have pierced Carl to the core for him to paint so many of them on the walls and ceiling.

There were white hand prints smeared on the wall. They were definitely creepy-looking. Then, near the far corner of the room, I saw the words to the song that the Carl actors sang the night we went to the festival. The white paint of the song's words dripped like white blood.

I read the words out loud as I stood there, mesmerized by Carl's song. Once again, the words made me feel deep emotions of sadness and regret.

Oh, Phantom of the woods, tell me your tale,
Of ancient secrets and nights so pale.
Lost in the mist, your presence is near,
Losing you is my ultimate fear.

Through tangled vines and whisper of trees,
The Phantom wanders, a silent breeze.
Eyes like stars, piercing through the night,
I cannot seem to win this fight.

Though I may fear the dark's embrace,
The Phantom beckons in this place.
But in its realm, there's solace found,
A sanctuary where peace resounds.

The walls also had the Phantom Buck's white antlers painted in multiple places. I thought of the buck I had seen earlier in the day and shook my head. The eyes and the antlers were identical to the ones Carl had painted over and over in this room and on the painting that hid this lair from his family.

"McKay, have you ever seen anything like this?" Jack asked.

He pointed at the floor in front of us. I broke my gaze from the walls and ceiling and looked down. I blinked over and over, trying to understand what I saw.

Almost the entire floor of the lair was covered with a diorama of the entire forest of Eerie Hollow. I got down on my knees and examined the floor. Thousands of tiny trees had been sculpted out of toothpicks, each tree different from the one next to it. He had sculpted hollows, hills, streams, and rock formations out of clay. He even had a replica of this very mansion and the pond next to it.

He had created a three-dimensional map of the entire area. It was intricate and detailed. I noticed that small white Xs had been drawn in different places. There was an X painted near the mansion's pond. I got down on my knees and looked closer. I gasped out loud when I realized what I saw.

"Jack, this white X is in the exact spot where he carved his name on the tree by the pond. I think something is written on the toothpick tree, but it's so small. I can't read it," I shared.

Jack looked around and spotted an old-fashioned magnifying glass wrapped in brass with a wooden handle. It had been left to gather dust on the edge of this masterpiece. He picked it up and brought it close to his mouth. He took a deep breath and blew. The dust flew off in a twisting cloud. He cleaned the glass with his shirt and then handed it to me.

I brought the magnifying glass to my eye and looked through it. Sure enough, the letters CARL were etched on the tiny toothpick tree in the tiniest writing.

"This is incredible," I said to myself.

Jack walked around the room, admiring Carl's workmanship.

"It's amazing how creative Carl was even though he was going nuts. This room is beyond imagination," he said.

"I agree. He was a creative genius like no other person I've ever known."

I paused for a moment. I noticed other white symbols painted on the diorama.

"Jack, look at all the different markings. What do you think they mean?"

The markings were spread throughout the Eerie Hollow forest. I brought the magnifying glass in to take a closer look. I knew they had to be important.

"Hey Jack, is there any paper lying around? I want to copy these symbols down."

He grabbed a little notebook in the corner of the floor, which had a little pencil next to it. He handed it to me. I carefully copied each symbol that I saw into the little notebook. It took some time to find them all and copy them down. Then I stood up, stretched my arms, and put the copy of the symbols in my pants pocket.

I looked over by the door and saw something that made me smile—boots. I walked over to them and picked them up. I remembered that Carl had hunted with nothing more than red wool socks to protect his feet. These had to be the boots Carl stopped wearing so the Phantom couldn't hear his footsteps.

Suddenly, the sound of the front door opening reached our ears. I dropped the boots in a panic. I didn't want the adults to see what we had found. This was Jack's and my secret now! Quickly, we turned off the lights, jumped outside the entrance, and closed the painting door. Jack locked the painting as fast as he could. I looked down and saw the net with the bells. We had to move it before my parents came up the stairs.

We picked it up. The bells started to jingle like Santa's sleigh. Jack and I looked at each other and started to run as fast as we could to the office with the bells bouncing noisily on the floor. We opened the office with the old, black key I kept in my front pants pocket. Then we threw the net and its noisy bells into the room.

I knew we were going to get caught, but then I had a great idea. I ripped a couple of bells off the net and ran out of the office, locking it behind me. I gave Jack a bell, and we ran to the end of the hallway. We jingled the bells as loud as we could.

Mom and Dad came up the stairs and looked at us like we were crazy.

"Why are you jingling those bells? Where did you even find them?" asked Dad.

"Oh, they were in our room. We were just playing a game to see who could be the loudest. Jack won," I lied.

Mom and Dad looked at us strangely. Then they kind of just shrugged their shoulders, walked past us, and opened the door to their room. They were carrying some stuff that they had bought in town.

When they came out of their room, they were both smiling and happy. I knew this was my chance to ask about hunting with Jack. If I've learned anything over my twelve years on this earth, it's that the best time to ask Mom and Dad anything is when they're in a good mood!

"Tomorrow is the opening day of rifle deer season. Can Jack and I go hunt together down behind our house?"

Mom and Dad looked at each other for a second.

"They have both hunted on their own before. I don't see a problem with it," Dad said as he nodded his approval to Mom.

He shot me a secret wink while Mom looked down, contemplating her answer.

"If Dallas is ok with it, I don't see why not. We have so much to do while Dallas is here to help. I don't think we will have much time to hunt this year. I know you two have really been looking forward to it," Mom said.

Jack and I jumped up and down with excitement. We ran over to Dallas, who was coming up the stairs, and asked him if Jack and I could hunt together in the morning.

"Of course you can! I hear there are some giant bucks in this area. Just today, I heard some older fellers going on and on about the giant-sized bucks that they had seen while scouting," said Dallas.

We yelled thank you as we ran down to our room to get some hunting stuff put together. We were going to go hunting! But not just any kind of hunting. We would be hunting The Phantom of Eerie Hollow....

Chapter 21

Flint and Steel

Once in our room, Jack and I grabbed our backpacks and started filling them with hunting supplies. I looked over and noticed Jack packing a neat-looking flint and steel.

"Hey, Jack! What's that? Can I see it?" I asked.

He handed it to me. My eyes got big with excitement. I turned the flint and steel over in my hand, studying it. The flint was very interesting. It was black and shaped like a rod. Hundreds of tiny silver scratches lined the rod that had been glued into a wooden handle. The handle had a hole with a string looped through it. A piece of steel hung from the string so that it would never get lost. A jagged half-moon was cut out of the steel so that it would slide perfectly down the rod, creating as much friction as possible. I looked closer at the wooden handle. The phrase True Hunter had been burned into it.

I smiled, then took the jagged end of the steel and ran it across the flint away from my body. A shower of sparks flew into the air and burned out harmlessly on their way to the floor. It was pretty neat. A burning metallic smell filled the room. I nodded with satisfaction and looked at the burnt inscription on the handle once more.

"What's True Hunter?" I asked curiously.

"Oh, it's a motto my grandpa created a long time ago to help my dad remember to hunt the right way. When my dad was just a boy, my grandpa gave him a brass compass as a birthday present. It had the motto True Hunter etched into the front. My dad kept it his whole life, but he ended up giving it to Sienna," he said.

"You mean the same Sienna that we called the other day? The girl that watched you shoot the ear off that grizzly?" I asked for clarification.

"Yes, that same Sienna. She used my dad's True Hunter compass to find the highway after Dad crashed our plane four years ago. She saved my Dad's life," he explained.

Jack paused for a moment, then reached into his pocket and pulled out a silver coin. He looked it over with sad eyes, then handed it to me carefully.

"Those were tough times for me. Before that hunting trip, my mom had just died. Dad gave me this coin before the hunt. He made it just for me and put that same motto on it. I carry it everywhere."

I looked at the coin closely. The face of the coin had a giant buck leaping out of a compass with the words True Hunter below. I was mesmerized by it. I turned the coin over and saw that on the back, there was a young hunter with an older hunter. The older hunter had his hand on the younger hunter's shoulder as they walked. The words "Your Legacy" were etched above them. Talk about something special. I could see why this coin meant so much to Jack.

I handed it back to him. He looked at it for a few seconds, then put it back in his pocket.

"So, I try my very best to remember to live by the True Hunter motto. I'm the one who burned True Hunter into the handle of my flint and steel," he explained, taking back the flint and steel and putting it into his bag.

He paused for a second and then looked me in the eyes.

"McKay, do you really think that buck you saw was the same Phantom Buck that made Carl go crazy?" Jack asked.

"I mean, it looked exactly like the buck in the painting. I don't know what else to say other than I would do anything to harvest that buck," I explained.

Jack nodded in a way that made me think that he might not really believe me, but it didn't matter. I knew I would do everything in my power to bring home the Phantom.

"I mean, if it is the same Phantom Buck, you don't think you'll go crazy too? Do you?" Jack asked, with some concern in his eyes.

"I'm sure I'll be fine," I replied.

I looked in my backpack and shook my head with disapproval.

"Jack, we are forgetting one of the most important things for a successful hunt," I said with a serious tone.

He tilted his head, showing me that he didn't know what I was referring to.

I looked Jack straight in the eyes and said, "Snacks... We don't have any snacks."

I tried really hard to keep the serious look on my face, but I couldn't help but bust out a giant, toothy smile. We laughed together and decided we needed to make our own trip into town and do some major snack shopping.

We opened the door to our room, and I yelled out for Mom. We watched as she skipped across the marble floor like a kid. She was obviously still in a great mood. I think this place made her happy. We all were happy here.

"Mom, can Jack and I go into town real quick and get some supplies for our hunt in the morning? I promise we will be back before dark."

She squinted her eyes and said, "Supplies? You mean snacks, don't you?

I nodded my head with a grin.

"At least you have learned something from your parents. Snacks are one of the best parts of hunting!" she exclaimed.

Jack and I laughed. We both knew that my mom and dad had a sweet tooth. They always had a stash of chocolate that they could eat at a moment's notice, and almost every night, they would share a pint of ice cream.

We went out the giant front door, and I hopped onto my bike. My dad was nice enough to let Jack borrow his bike.

We raced each other to the grocery store. The crisp November air made me shiver a little. Jack grabbed some chocolate chip cookies in the store, and I grabbed a bag of BBQ potato chips. Jack looked over at me like I was crazy and snatched the bag of chips out of my hand.

"What are you doing?" I asked with a look of confusion running across my forehead.

"Are you kidding me? That bag will make more noise than a raccoon in a metal trash can. Deer will hear you snacking a mile away. Get something quieter," Jack demanded.

I realized that he was right and grabbed a box of donuts. Then, we loaded up with candy bars. We hopped back on our bikes and headed home. On the way home, we ran into a familiar face.

Chapter 22

Map Symbols

"McKay! Hey! It's good to see you!" exclaimed Stan.

"Hi, Stan!" I replied with a bit of excitement.

"Looks like you two boys just bought every snack in the grocery store," Stan said with a laugh.

"Well, tomorrow is the rifle opener. We had to make sure we were properly prepared to go hunt some giant bucks," I joked back.

Just then, a couple of old men burst out of the pub and took a few steps into the street. They were quite the pair. One of them was tall, skinny, and bald as a golf ball. The other was quite short, very round in the midsection, and had long, greasy, gray hair. They kind of looked like the number 10 when they stood next to one another!

They stumbled over to an old, blue, beat-up pickup truck. They were pretty shady-looking characters if you were to ask me. I looked up at Stan, and he shook his head in disappointment.

"The Creedy brothers. Skeeter and Tick. Named after the area's notorious blood-sucking insects by their loving mother (Stan coughed when he said "loving"). Skeeter is the tall one with the long nose, and Tick is the round one with short legs. They have been the biggest blemish on this town for the past fifty years," bemoaned Stan.

My ears perked up, and my eyebrows jumped.

"Wait, did you say 'The Creedy Brothers'?" I blurted out quickly.

"Ya. Do you know of them?" Stan asked.

"They are the ones that Great-Grandpa Willie mentioned in his journal. The bullies that made fun of Carl the night he cursed the town," I replied hastily.

"So, you did find Willie's journal—you clever boy. Willie told me you would. He told me all I needed to do was get you that old key, and you would find the journal," Stan said with a twinkling in his eye.

"Ya, we found it. Ol' secret drawer in the desk routine," I said, trying to sound smart.

Stan smiled and nodded a congratulatory look. Then he looked back over at the Creedy boys. Dark smoke billowed out of the exhaust of their truck as they drove down the street.

"Yes, you are correct. Those are the men who taunted Carl relentlessly about his Phantom Buck. They are the ones we portrayed in the little skit the other night. We never say their names in the skit, but everyone in town knows who they are. They are the worst kind of people. Always lying and cheating, but worse than that, they are poachers," Stan explained.

"I hate poachers. We see poachers all the time in Alaska. Nothing makes me more angry than seeing a poacher," added Jack.

"They've been bragging about seeing a giant buck for weeks now. I bet you they have been out in the woods with a spotlight trying to get him," Stan said with disgust.

I gulped. Fear ripped through my chest. I really hoped they weren't talking about the Phantom Buck. I would cry if that buck fell at the hands of awful poachers.

"Hey Stan, it was nice running into you. We've got to get home, though," I said.

I put my hand in my pocket. My hands slipped by the paper I had used to draw the different symbols from the 3D map on the floor of Carl's lair.

"One more thing. Umm. Stan. Umm. Do these symbols mean anything to you?" I asked as I gave him the piece of paper.

He looked at them closely. Then he looked at me with a grin.

"Where did you find these symbols?" he asked.

"Oh, umm, nowhere. They were just on an old map, and I wondered if you knew what they meant," I said.

I was trying my best not to lie but not tell all of the truth.

"They are hunting symbols. Ol' Carl used to make hunting maps and use these symbols to show where certain things were in the woods. If you've got one of his old hunting maps, it's worth its weight in gold. Carl knew these woods better than anyone! He used to show me his maps at the end of each hunting season. For example, this chair-looking symbol means a tree stand. This Y-looking symbol means a funnel through which deer travel. You know, like a natural pinch point where trails converge between two fields," Stan explained.

He went down the list and told me what each one meant. It was quite the list. He had a symbol for everything: Bedding Area, Rubs, Water Hole, Scrapes, Feeding Area, Acorns, and Antler Sheds. Stan did get stuck on one symbol.

"I'm not too sure what this flying bird symbol means. Strange. Maybe he saw a quail or pheasant or something. I don't know. Where did you find this map?" he asked.

I grinned as I hopped on my bike and started riding off. I turned my head back towards Stan as I sped away.

"I found it in the walls of the mansion! It may just be that adventure you promised me!" I hollered.

Chapter 23

Going Hunting

The rest of the evening went pretty smoothly. We had dinner, and then Jack and I decided we should probably go to bed early since we would get up before dawn. My parents smiled as we left to go to bed so early. Dad turned to Mom and Dallas and said, "Maybe we should let them go hunting year-round. Then maybe they would go to bed early every night."

They all laughed, but I wasn't going to give him the pleasure of laughing at such a lame dad joke.

Although, I guess I could see it from their point of view. Usually, we are fighting to stay up as late as possible, but not tonight. We had an adventure waiting for us early the next morning. We jumped straight into bed and didn't even talk.

However, I wasn't able to sleep. I couldn't stop thinking about those awful Creedy old men. I thought about how they bullied Carl all those years ago. Nobody deserves to be bullied. Nobody. Then I thought about the idea of them poaching the Phantom. It made my blood boil. A deer like that deserved to be memorialized forever. Not shot in the dark with a spotlight and hidden from the world.

Finally, I fell asleep. I slept like a log until Jack's snoring woke me up at two in the morning. I love Jack and all, but his snoring was not of a heavenly nature and was probably the worst sound I had ever heard. I sat up as I remembered what Stan said about a hunting map of Carl's. He said it was worth its weight in gold. I laughed because the map in his lair probably weighed thousands of pounds. That's a lot of gold.

I decided it would be wise to make a copy of the map to take with us on our hunt, so I snuck out of the bedroom and left Jack to his snoring. I crept up the dark stairs and made my way to the lair. I almost jumped when I saw the Phantom Buck's eyes in the painting. It seemed like they were glowing as they watched me put the tiny key into the cave keyhole. The painting door quietly opened.

I took a step into the lair and shut it silently behind me. I turned on the Christmas lights. The white eyes on the walls lit up eerily in the light. It was all so terrifyingly beautiful. I grabbed a blank sheet of paper and did my best to copy the map to scale. Obviously, my map didn't do Carl's map justice, but it would at least give us an idea of where to start. I made sure I included every single symbol that had been marked on his map.

I swear I heard a whisper as I turned off the lights and closed the painting door behind me. I opened the painting door again and listened, but I didn't hear anything at all except my heavy breathing. I shook my head in frustration and closed the painting again.

This time, I heard, as clear as day, a whisper that said, "Find me." I freaked out a little bit. I looked up at the eyes in the painting. They were glowing bright white and were looking straight at me. I tripped backwards and fell to the ground. I ran down the stairs, swung my bedroom door open, and turned on the lights.

"What in the world are you doing, McKay? Can't a guy sleep in peace around here?" groaned Jack.

"Jack, get up. I swear I just heard a voice coming from Carl's lair. It said, 'Find me'. I'm totally freaking out," I said, with a voice full of panic.

Jack shook his head and got up. He put his hand on my shoulder. I calmed down a bit. We went up the stairs together and opened the lair. We heard nothing, absolutely nothing. We closed the painting door and heard nothing. Jack looked at me like I might be going crazy, but I knew what I had heard.

Jack looked at his watch. It was now three in the morning.

"Well, I guess since we're already up, we might as well make our way into the woods," he suggested.

We grabbed our backpacks full of supplies, snacks, and our trusty guns. We were careful to make sure our guns weren't loaded, and then we quietly opened the front door and made our way out into the darkness. It was chilly, for sure, but my adrenaline was still going strong and kept me warm.

We walked down to where Carl had carved his name into the tree. I pulled the map out of my pocket and showed it to Jack. He thought I was pretty smart for making a copy of the map. We found the X that marked this exact tree.

"What should we do?" I asked.

Jack helped Dallas with his guiding business in Alaska and was pretty good at making hunting game plans. I wasn't too prideful to take advantage of his wealth of hunting knowledge.

"I think we should go check out this place where it says he has a tree stand. Maybe the tree stand is still there. It looks like it is set up within shooting distance of this funnel. In my opinion, that would be a great place to start," Jack explained.

I nodded my head in agreement. According to the map, we would need to cross a dirt road south of us and then follow a small stream until it forked. We began walking in that general direction. We followed little trails made by forest animals. It was the best way to cut through the forest as efficiently as possible. We walked for a good hour or so and finally found the dirt road.

We crossed the road and kept our ears open for the sound of running water. It didn't look like it would be too far from the road. Suddenly, we heard the rumbling sound of an old truck engine. We instinctively ducked down and turned our attention to the road. The sound of a beat-up truck slowly got louder and louder. Then, a light appeared down the road.

Anger shot through my veins as I realized that the light that we saw was a spotlight. The truck slowly passed us by. I saw the bald head and long nose of the man driving the truck. It was Skeeter Creedy and his short brother Tick, looking to poach a giant buck illegally in the dark of night. Jack shook his head in disgust. I clenched my teeth with rage. The sound of a tin can bouncing off the dirt road made its way to our ears. Not only were they poachers, but they were throwing trash into the woods. These guys were the absolute worst.

"Those no good, poaching fools throwing their empty cans out into the woods," I said with disgust.

"I hate it too, but there's nothing we can do about it. Let's just get to the spot where the treestand is supposed to be," Jack said.

There were leaves everywhere, so it was hard to stay silent, but we walked as quietly as we could. We tried to step on solid things like rocks and tree roots to avoid the crunching of the leaves. My dad had taught me that trick to being quiet last deer season. Jack would walk ten steps or so, then stop and listen. He was quite skilled. I was pretty impressed by his hunting abilities.

Jack stopped for a moment and pointed to a small tree.

"Notice anything special," he asked.

"Umm, not really. Why? What's so special about this tree?" I asked.

"It's not the tree. It's what's below the tree. Look at how the ground is all torn up. This is a scrape. Do you see the licking branch about five feet high? Every buck that comes through here will tear up the ground a bit and lick that branch to leave their unique scent. Then, when other bucks lick that branch, they are able to learn which bucks are hanging out in this area. This is a good sign that we are in a good place to harvest a big buck," he explained.

I nodded to show him that I understood what he was saying. It was amazing to me that deer could learn so much from a licked branch.

After walking a while longer, we heard the sound of running water. Once we got to the stream, we followed it until it forked off like the map had said it would. Then we angled our way to where Carl had marked his treestand on the map. It was still dark, so it was hard to see anything, let alone an old treestand up in some tree. We had been walking for a while when we stopped to take a breath. I leaned my hand against an old tree as I rested for a quick second.

Suddenly, I felt something tickle the hand that was on the tree. I slowly looked at my hand in the moonlight. A giant spider was crawling down the backside of it. I ripped my hand from the tree and shook it violently. As I whipped my hand around, my face landed smack dab in the middle of its huge spider web. I grabbed at my face as I flung my body around in circles. The sticky spider web clung to my skin. Then, suddenly, I felt Jack grab my shoulders. He held me still for a moment and told me to calm down. I felt him carefully remove the spider web from my face.

I slowly opened my eyes to see him looking right at me. We both smiled. Then he lifted his head to laugh silently. As he looked up, I watched the smile on his face change into a look of awe and wonder....

Chapter 24

Rifle Tower

Jack looked at me with a sparkle in his eye. He reached out and grabbed my head firmly with his cold hands. He didn't say a word as he tilted my gaze toward the sky. Once I saw it, I also felt awe and wonder. The most magnificent treestand I had ever seen had been built up high in the giant oak tree.

Jack walked to the back side of the giant tree and whispered to me to come over to where he was standing. I walked over to him and saw that the tree's limbs made a perfect ladder to the treestand. Jack grinned, put his bag down, and started climbing. Within seconds, Jack was sitting in the treestand. He waved at me to come on up.

I didn't hesitate. I quickly worked my way up the branches of the tree. When I got to the stand, Jack reached out his hand and pulled me in. The stand was made out of a six-foot by six-foot platform built on two thick limbs of the tree. Walls had been built on the platform as well. There was even a roof that had kept the stand dry. It had protected it from rot for all these years.

I had never been in a stand like this before. Talk about luxury... Carl knew how to hunt in style! The stand was at least thirty-five years old but still sturdy. Carl had not cut any corners crafting this stand.

Two old wooden chairs were sitting side by side. Jack and I sat down carefully. We nodded our heads together in unison. This was the place where we would hunt today. Jack made his way back down the tree limbs and came back with our packs. Then he went back down two more times to retrieve our rifles. He was absolutely silent. He sat down next to me. I patted him on the shoulder to thank him for bringing my gun and gear up to me. We loaded our rifles and put the safeties on. Then we sat in silence, waiting for the first signs of light.

It has always amazed me how carefully the sun rises. The darkness begins to fade almost imperceptibly. Slowly, things you couldn't see before come into the light. I watched all around to see what I could see next. First, it was the closest trees, then the shape of the meadow, and finally, I could see the funnel of trees that ran between the two meadows in front of us. This tree-stand seemed to be in the perfect spot.

I focused on that tiny strip of trees. Jack whispered to me that deer like to stay in the tree line before coming out to feed. He also said that deer would most likely take their time making sure it was safe before coming into the open. Luckily, this tree stand did a fantastic job hiding Jack and me from being seen. There was no way a deer could see us behind the walls of this stand.

Suddenly, I noticed something moving in the tree line. I grabbed my binoculars out of my bag. I pulled them up to my eyes and focused on the spot where I saw the movement. It wasn't a deer. It was a raccoon. I watched the raccoon for a few minutes.

I have always thought the mask around a raccoon's eyes was so funny. It's like nature knew that raccoons would always be up to no good and needed to be dressed up for mischief. I watched as he pulled his little black hands up to his face. I laughed inside my head as I imagined him actually wearing a mask and black leather gloves.

As the sun slowly rose, I was able to see everything clearly. I took my eyes off the tree line for a moment and looked at the inside walls of the tree stand. It was old and gray. It had been painted black once upon a time. That paint probably helped keep the wood in such good condition. I looked above the slit that had been cut out for us to watch the fields. It had two names carved into the wood. Carl and Cliff.

The two names next to each other made me feel happy inside. I tried to imagine Grandpa Cliff sitting next to his playful twin brother while they waited for big bucks to show themselves. I wondered what kind of tricks Carl would play on his brother while they sat up here patiently waiting for giant bucks.

I noticed that "Rifle Tower" had been carved deep into the wood above their names. I smiled at the play on words. The Eiffel Tower in France was such a beautifully built landmark. They must have laughed as they thought of names to name this treestand. To the brothers, this treestand was probably just as fancy as the Eiffel Tower. The name Rifle Tower was perfect.

Just then, I noticed Jack reach into his backpack. He pulled out a grunt tube and some old antler sheds. He winked at me and then put the grunt tube to his mouth. He made a deep grunt sound. It kind of sounded like a burp, but that's what big bucks sound like during the rut. He grunted a couple of times, then took the antler sheds and started pounding them together as if they were two big bucks in the fight of their lives over a mature doe.

I watched the field in front of us to see if there was any movement. Then, a deer appeared out of nowhere, looking around for the big fight we were imitating with the antlers. I looked through my binoculars and saw that it was a buck. He was a small four-point buck with two points on each side that looked like little forks.

I pointed toward the small buck to show Jack what he had called in. He smiled back at me and put a doe call up to his lips. He made the whiney sound of a doe in heat. The buck looked around and trotted towards

us, entering the open meadow. He seemed to be looking straight past the big oak we were sitting in.

He stopped in the middle of the meadow and hung
out for a little while as he snacked on some crisp grass.
Then he disappeared into the trees.

"He will be a good one in a couple of years. Best to
let 'em grow for now," I whispered to Jack.

I felt kind of mature saying that. It sounded like
something my dad would say, but the reality is, if today
was the last day of the season, that buck would have
been mine for sure.

I noticed a couple of does walking through the funnel of trees. I looked closely, but there weren't any
bucks with them. Jack did another grunt, but this time,
he made a wheezing sound after it.

"Big ol' bucks like to wheeze after they grunt," Jack
explained.

I grabbed the antler sheds and went to work. It was
fun pretending to be a big buck fighting another buck.
We sat and watched. Then I noticed some movement
in the treeline....

Chapter 25

Bad Shot

I wanted it so badly to be the Phantom Buck that I had seen a couple of days prior. I wanted Jack to see its white eyes and antlers. I needed him to see him. If Jack sees the Phantom, then I wouldn't feel so alone and crazy thinking that it was the same buck that had driven Carl to Crazy Town.

Jack and I both pulled out our binoculars. The deer was still pretty deep in the trees. Slowly, the deer moved closer to the tree line. At first, I couldn't tell if it was a doe or a buck. It had a big body, for sure. Finally, after a few minutes, his antlers came into view.

It was a buck, and he was a good one! He slowly walked back and forth in the tree line. He had his eyes fixed in our direction. He was looking for the buck that made that grunt and wheeze.

Jack and I both pulled our rifles up to the slit in the treestand. We rested them on the old wood. I tried to find the buck in my scope but struggled.

"Do you see him, Jack?" I whispered.

"Ya, I found him in my scope, but I don't have a clear shot. He's a shooter, but I'm not going to shoot through a bunch of brush," said Jack.

I finally found him in my scope. I saw his antlers. He definitely wasn't the Phantom Buck. His antlers didn't have any drop tines and his eyes were dark, not white. I counted nine total points. Four on one side and five on the other. A trophy for sure, but not the trophy I wanted.

"Well, he's yours if you can get a shot," I whispered to Jack.

The buck didn't move a muscle. He just stood there staring. I began to grow impatient.

"Just take the shot, Jack. The bullet will make it through the bushes. No one is going to know that it's not a clear shot. He's spooked. He knows something is wrong and isn't going to come out. Now's your only chance," I whispered.

"I would know. I would know that I took a bad shot," Jack replied.

Then, just like I predicted, the buck lost his patience. He didn't see what he thought he should, and he walked away from the treeline back into the forest.

Jack looked over at me and shook his head. The opportunity had been lost.

He lowered his head for a second, then whispered, "McKay, I've seen hunters take bad shots through brush. It's not fair to the animals. I've followed blood trails for miles never to find them. It breaks my heart every time I think about the animal suffering because some hunter thought it was his only chance to get a shot."

Jack was right. I felt terrible inside for even having the thought to take a bad shot. I looked down at Jack's hands. He was turning the True Hunter coin over and over in his right hand. He seemed to really take that concept to heart.

We sat there in silence for a couple of hours. Neither of us spoke. The sun got higher and higher in the sky. We didn't see another deer that morning. Jack reached into his bag and pulled out a sandwich.

"Well, I'm guessing the morning hunt is about over. The deer will most likely be on their way to bed down for the warm part of the day," explained Jack.

We discussed it and decided to stay in the Rifle Tower for the rest of the day. We didn't want to leave this perfect spot. I pulled out the map, and we studied it quietly. These woods were full of hollows. There were so many places for big deer to hide. If we were to walk around now, we would most likely jump them from their bedding spots, never to see them again.

As we sat quietly, I closed my eyes. I totally fell asleep. I napped for what seemed to be a few minutes when suddenly I felt an elbow in my side.

"McKay, wake up. It's deer hunting time. I've been doe calling for half an hour already," Jack whispered.

I opened my eyes and saw that the sun was on its way down. I smiled at Jack.

"Guess I slept the day away. There is nothing in this world as wholesome as a long nap while hunting in the woods," I whispered.

"My dad doesn't let me nap while we're hunting. He claims that I snore too loud and that I would scare off anything within two miles of me. I don't buy it, though. I've never heard myself snore," claimed Jack.

I looked at him like he had two heads. I shook my head side to side in disbelief.

"Jack. Your snore is louder than a pack of a hundred hyenas laughing at the top of their lungs. Your snore is louder than the rocket that took men to the moon this past summer. Your snore is louder than a," I was cut off by the sound of antlers crashing into one another....

Chapter 26

Fighting Bucks

Jack and I both whipped our heads in the direction of the sound. My heart started thumping and pumping at full throttle as I saw two giant bucks fighting in the meadow directly in front of us. Dirt flew in the air as each buck fought with all their might.

"They must have snuck in while you were talking about my snoring," whispered Jack.

"Holy Moly! They are huge!" I whispered back.

We grabbed our rifles and got into position. The bucks were so close that we could hear their heavy breathing.

Antlers clicked and clacked as swollen necks dripped with sweat. These were big, dominant bucks. With all my heart, I hoped that one of them was the Phantom, but it was too hard to get a clean look at either set of antlers. Their antlers were meshed together as each buck maneuvered with their hind legs. I looked through my scope, and Jack looked through his. What an epic story this would be if we shot them both at the same time while they were in mortal combat.

I clicked my safety off and put my finger gently on the trigger of my trusty rifle. Jack did the same.

"McKay, let's wait until they are both broadside and not moving. I'll take whichever one is on the left, and you can take the one on the right. Shoot on my count of three," Jack instructed.

The big bucks disengaged antlers for a moment, then crashed into each other once again. Their heads almost touched the ground, trying to gain the advantage over the other. They weren't broadside yet. One of them had his white tail pointed straight at us. I tried so hard to see if one of them was the Phantom, but I still couldn't tell. I watched as they quickly switched positions. Now, the other buck had his tail facing me.

I looked at their antlers again. They were thick, dark, and tall. I remembered that the Phantom Buck had bone-white antlers. My heart sank when I realized that neither of these bucks was him, but both of these bucks were bigger than any buck my parents had ever shot. I couldn't let this opportunity pass. I was going to shoot, even if it wasn't the Phantom.

I watched closely through my scope as one of the bucks twisted his antlers downward with such strength that the other buck flipped over. The buck landed on his back but jumped up quickly. The fallen buck's eyes filled with deep intensity, and he charged the other buck, pushing him backward. These bucks were studs, and neither of them wanted to lose.

Just then, they rotated, so they were both perfectly broadside to us. I put the crosshairs behind the shoulder of the buck on the right. I could see his muscles bulging with sweat dripping down his leg. I breathed deeply. I calmed myself the best I possibly could. At that moment, the bucks stopped moving completely.

"One, Two, Three..." Jack counted.

I aimed at a single hair behind his front shoulder. Jack and I both pulled the triggers to our rifles at the exact same time. A loud bang rang through the woods. The buck on the left dropped in his tracks, pulling the buck on the right to the ground with him. Their antlers were still locked together. The buck on the right shook his head violently and disengaged his tangled antlers. He stood up with a snort and bounded off unscathed. I blinked my eyes in disbelief. I looked at Jack, and then I looked at my rifle. It never fired....

I felt sick to my stomach. How could this have happened? I wanted to puke in frustration. On the other hand, Jack jumped up and down with excitement from dropping his trophy in its tracks.

I grabbed the bolt to my rifle and pulled it back, ejecting the shell onto the Rifle Tower's wooden floor. I reached down and picked it up. The bullet was still in the brass casing. I looked at the primer. It had a dent in it from the firing pin of the rifle. Usually, that would mean that the bullet had been shot, but not in this case, I guess. For some reason, the primer didn't create the spark to set the gunpowder inside the shell on fire. That fire is what should have propelled my bullet towards that buck. I shook my head as I showed Jack the evidence that I had indeed pulled the trigger.

"A misfire? I'm so sorry, McKay. That is some bad luck right there," Jack sympathized.

The woods fell silent. I followed Jack down the tree. We slowly walked up to his trophy buck. The meadow floor was completely torn up from the epic fight. Jack walked behind his buck and pushed the end of his rifle into the magnificent buck's neck. No movement.

I tried to smile and be happy for Jack and this great moment, but I felt cheated. I walked over to the big oak tree and watched Jack grab his buck by its giant set of antlers. Jack's white smile lit up the forest. Then I watched as Jack bowed his head and whispered something into the ears of his trophy buck. I looked in Jack's hands and saw his True Hunter coin. He was rubbing it over and over.

Maybe this was Jack's reward for not taking that bad shot earlier. Maybe I was reaping the consequence of trying to get Jack to take a bad shot. I didn't know what to think. I just sat there holding the misfired cartridge in my hand.

Jack counted the dark chocolate-colored points of his trophy buck. There were six on the left and six on the right. He was a true mainframe twelve-pointer—a trophy buck by anyone's standards. I felt jealousy fill my chest. I didn't want to feel it, but I did. It wasn't fair. I should have been holding a trophy buck's antlers in my hands, too.

After a few moments, Jack stood up and came over to me. He was smiling big. Adrenaline was still coursing through his veins. He paused for a second before speaking to me. I could tell he was trying to think of the best thing to say to his depressed cousin.

"McKay, sometimes bad things happen. But I can't help but wonder if this was meant to be. If you had shot that big buck, your hunt would be over, and you wouldn't be able to chase the Phantom Buck you saw."

He sounded so wise. I thought for a moment. Jack made an excellent point. I looked at the misfired cartridge and realized that maybe it was meant to be. I cracked a smile and got up. I hugged Jack and pounded his back with my fist like grown-up men do. I told him congratulations on his trophy. I snapped out of my momentary depression and gave Jack the praise that he deserved for making such a great shot in such a tense situation. It really was an epic moment. A moment that I would not be forgetting anytime soon.

We knew we needed to process his buck quickly. Darkness began to overtake the light of the forest. A creepy fog slowly worked into the meadow where Jack's trophy lay still. An eerie feeling fell over us. Neither of us wanted to admit it, but a tinge of fear crept into our bodies. Jack began working on his buck. I knelt down and held the hind legs open for him.

I looked into the treeline and was startled by what I saw. Penetrating white eyes were staring right at me. In the moonlight, I saw the double drop tine antlers. It was the Phantom Buck. I stared for a moment. Then, I turned quickly to get Jack's attention. I whispered for him to look as I let go of the buck's hind legs. I pointed towards the Phantom, but to my frustration, the Phantom had vanished. Jack once again did not see him. I reached into my pocket and felt the misfired cartridge. At that moment, I knew destiny had bigger plans for me.

After processing Jack's buck, we each grabbed a side of the trophy buck's antlers and took our first steps toward home. Oh man, talk about hard work! That buck was heavy. I actually began to feel a bit relieved that I hadn't shot that other buck. That would have created twice the work.

We pulled and tugged on the buck's antlers, dragging his large body through the forest. We dragged that buck non-stop until the sound of a distant harmonica carried in the chilly breeze. Jack and I both stopped in our tracks. We peered into the darkness in the direction of the harmonica's song. We both gulped. It was in the same direction that I had seen the Phantom. Adrenaline came rushing into our twelve-year-old bodies, and we suddenly had the strength of grown men.

We started to run. We drug that heavy buck as if he were just a little doe. Before we knew it, we were crossing the dirt road. We continued to run. We made it probably fifty yards off the road when the sound of the Creedy's beat-up truck broke the forest's silence.

Chapter 27

Creedy Campsite

We quickly hid behind a bush. The truck came into view, this time coming from the opposite direction as before. We watched as a beam of light broke the darkness. It searched the forest for any sign of life. I hoped with all my heart that the Phantom Buck had moved far, far away from the potential grasp of the spotlight.

I got angry. Really, really angry. I wanted to stand up and throw a rock at their truck. I wanted to give those no-good poachers a piece of my mind. Someone needed to stand up to them and put an end to their pathetic, illegal poaching ways.

The truck passed, and darkness once again consumed the light. I looked at Jack and shook my head in disgust.

"Someone needs to make them stop their poaching," I said, with venom in my voice.

"Do you think they are camped out there?" asked Jack.

"I bet you they are. I bet they sleep during the day, get up when it's dark, and then poach all night," I said.

I paused for a moment as a mischievous plot popped into my mind.

"Jack, let's find their camp. They won't be back until morning. Now's the time," I said as I began walking towards the road.

Jack looked at me with wide eyes, trying to understand what I was thinking. A grin came over his face. He quickly covered his trophy buck with some brush. Luckily, there was a chill in the air to keep the meat cool. He followed me downhill towards the dirt road. When we got to the road, we piled a few rocks on top of each other to mark this spot. That way, we could make sure we would be able to get back to his buck. Then we started jogging down the side of the dirt road in the direction that the truck had come from.

We ran for maybe ten minutes when suddenly we smelled smoke. Their camp had to be nearby. We followed the tire tracks made by their truck. The tracks turned off the dirt road and into the woods. We found their messy camp. These guys were absolute pigs. Beer cans were strewn about carelessly. Candy wrappers covered the camp. They slept under a wind-torn, blue tarp that they had tied to four trees. Damp, dirty pillows, and crusty, old, moldy blankets lay on the makeshift tent's floor.

"These guys are disgusting," Jack groaned as the smell of their latrine made its way to our noses.

My heart sank as I saw a pile of antlers. These worthless excuses for men had cut the antlers off at least ten bucks. I looked through them to see what poor bucks they had shot.

"Do these guys only take the antlers?" I asked.

"Yep, they cut the antlers off and leave the body to rot. All they care about are the antlers," Jack explained.

I looked around their camp making mental notes in my mind.

"Jack, we are going to make these guys pay for what they did to Carl all those years ago. We're going to make them pay for all the bucks they've poached over the years. Mark my words. They will never step foot in Eerie Hollow's forest ever again."

I motioned to Jack for us to go. We jogged back down the roadside. We were careful not to leave any footprints. We found Jack's trophy buck right where we left him and dragged him the rest of the way to the mansion home. My soul was filled with energy as I thought of ways to scare the living daylights out of the old Creedy brothers.

When we got home, we threw open the large oak front door, took a few steps inside, and then began singing at the top of our lungs a little song we had prepared for this exact moment:

Big Buck Down
Big Buck Down
Bet ya didn't think we would get a
Big Buck Down

Mom, Dad, and Dallas came quickly down the stairs together. They were so happy and excited for us. We brought them outside and showed them Jack's trophy buck.

"Squirt! Would you look at that? What a memory! Tell us all about it!" Dallas said as he gave Jack a giant bear hug.

Jack dazzled everyone with his story, and then we worked together to hang Jack's buck out in the cold. This buck would definitely turn into yummy meals.

Chapter 28

Prank Planning

Early the next morning, I nudged Jack and woke him before the adults had gotten up.

"Let's go to Carl's Lair. We've got some planning to do," I said mischievously.

He got up and followed me up the stairs. We made our way to the painting and opened it. We snuck into the lair and shut the painting behind us.

"What has gotten into you, McKay? What planning are you talking about?" asked Jack.

"The old Creedy brothers tormented Carl all those years ago. I think it's about time for Carl to get some payback," I said as I rubbed my chin with my right hand.

"I say we go out into the woods tonight and help Carl play some pranks on those dirty old men," I said with a villain-like laugh.

I proceeded to tell Jack my plan. He laughed at every prank that I shared. It wouldn't be easy, but I was pretty sure we could scare the stink off of those Creedy brothers. After I shared my plans, Jack opened the painting and snuck out. As I turned off the light and stepped out of the lair, I swear I heard a laugh come from the walls of Carl's hideout. I took it as approval from Carl himself.

We went up into the attic and grabbed Carl's prank box. We went around the house and grabbed a few other special goodies. Then we went to our parents and asked if it would be alright if we camped out for two nights. We told them it was so we could get a little deeper into the woods for the morning hunt. I pushed my bottom lip out like I was sad that I hadn't gotten a buck yet. I made the best puppy eyes I could. Mom couldn't resist my puppy eyes.

"Fine. Two nights and two nights only. You can hunt all day after your second night in the woods, but you better be home that night, or you better believe I'll have the whole town out looking for you two!" she warned.

"Thanks, Mom, you're the best!" I replied.

We grabbed a tent and all our supplies and headed out. We laughed and giggled all the way down the first hollow. We passed the dirt road and set up camp deep in the woods, a good distance from the Creedy campsite. The sun began to set, and we knew we needed to hurry. The Creedy boys would be leaving to poach at any moment. I told Jack to grab his binoculars, and we headed over to the Creedy campsite.

"Shhhh, time to go into ninja mode. They can't know we are watching them," I whispered as we crested a small hill that overlooked their campsite.

We looked through our binoculars and found both Creedy pigs sleeping under the blue tarp. They looked like pretty sound sleepers. I mean, if they could sleep all day out in the woods with the sun up, they had to be.

Tick began to stir. His long, greasy, gray hair was stuck to his face. The sun had just set, and it was getting darker by the minute. Then Skeeter Creedy stretched out his long arms and sat up. He punched Tick in the arm and told him to get up. They both stood up and took a few steps out of their tent.

They grabbed their coffee, which was sitting over the fire. They each drank a cup, stoked the fire, and put the coffee kettle back on the fire. I guessed they hoped to keep it warm for the morning when they returned. When it was completely dark, they grabbed their .270 rifles and jumped into the truck. Then they drove off.

Again, my blood boiled at the thought of them poaching the Phantom Buck. When their truck was out of sight, we snuck down to their campsite to begin Phase One of my plan to scare the stink off the Creedys.

Once we got to their campsite, I took my backpack off, and we went to work. We put out carefully thought-out tricks and pranks to welcome the Creedy brothers back from their awful poaching antics. We covered our tracks. Then, we went back to our camp to get some sleep.

We hopped out of our sleeping bags early the next morning when it was still dark. We snuck over to the Creedy camp and got into position....

Chapter 29

Phase One

The Creedy brother's truck came down the dirt road right on queue. It was still dark, but the sun would be rising soon. The brothers got out of their truck, swearing and cursing about their failed poaching expedition. I signaled Jack, who had set up on the other side of the hill behind the Creedy campsite. Jack pulled out a harmonica. He put it to his lips and slowly blew into it.

I watched as the sound fell upon Skeeter and Tick Creedy's ears. They looked at each other and then in the direction they thought the sound came from.

"What in the world was that?" Skeeter said out loud.

"It was probably just the wind," reasoned Tick.

I watched as they headed toward the campfire. I pulled out my harmonica and carefully blew into it. The eerie sound reached the Creedys a second time, but this time from a different direction. They stopped in their tracks and looked towards my position.

Skeeter began shaking as he stuttered, "I uh, I uh, I know I heard it that time. That's Carl's bedeviled harmonica. It sounds closer than it ever has in the past."

At that exact moment, Tick plopped down into his lawn chair next to the fire. The sound of a juicy toot escaped his seat. Skeeter laughed as he pointed at Tick.

"The beans from last night must be gettin' to you. Best be checkin' your drawers," he hollered.

Tick stood up as quickly as he had sat down. He looked down at his chair and saw a Whoopee Cushion. He picked it up and scratched his head.

"Did you put this confounded whoopee cushion on my chair?" he snarled.

Skeeter shook his head violently.

"No, it wasn't me."

I watched closely through my binoculars as Tick brought the Whoopee Cushion closer to his face. The light from the fire illuminated the name CARL. The name was written on the toot-maker in black marker. The brother dropped it as if it was a thousand degrees. He gulped. I signaled Jack once more. He blew into his harmonica.

"It's Carl after all these years. It's Crazy Carl," declared Tick.

"Oh, don't be jumpin' to no conclusions. It ain't Crazy Carl," retorted Skeeter.

He reached down into his bag of Milk Duds and grabbed a handful. He stuffed them into his mouth. I watched closely as he bit down on his little snack. He chewed quickly. Then, his mouth slowed to a halt. I watched as disgust took over his facial muscles. He put his hand out and spit the halfway chewed matter into his open palm to take a closer look. He sniffed it...

"Deer poop! Someone put deer poop in my Milk Duds!" yelled Skeeter.

I started rolling on the forest floor, trying not to laugh out loud. I knew the deer poop would get a strong reaction! I thought about how it must have felt to chomp down and taste some fresh, juicy deer droppings. I'm guessing Skeeter didn't own a toothbrush, either. Carl would be so proud of me.

Tick reached over the fire and poured Skeeter a cup of coffee to wash out the poop taste. His hand shook as he poured. He peered into the darkness as if looking for a ghost.

Skeeter lifted the coffee mug to his lips and took a giant swig. Immediately, he spit it out all over Tick's face. Tick licked his chapped lips.

"That ain't no coffee! That's hot orange juice!"

The brothers immediately realized what he said. Skeeter and Tick's eyes got huge, and their eyebrows pulled tight.

"That was one of Crazy Carl's favorite tricks," Skeeter said as he started to shake violently with fear.

I blew into my harmonica once more. The sound carried to the shaking brothers. My timing was perfect. The brothers began to panic. Their erratic breathing and darting eyes proved that they were totally flustered.

"Let's just get some shut-eye. We just ain't thinkin' straight," Tick suggested as he searched the darkness for answers.

Skeeter nodded and headed over to the latrine. He dropped his drawers and took a step closer to the hole dug to hold their number ones and number twos, if you know what I mean... As he stepped, his foot landed on the trigger mechanism for Carl's fake rattlesnake. The spring released, sending the snake's head right into Skeeter's butt cheek. Skeeter jumped and twisted around in circles. With his pants still down around his skinny ankles, he fell backwards, right into the stinky, nasty hole in the ground. He hopped up and tried to run as the fake snake rattled. He tripped over his pants and fell flat on his face.

He rolled around on the ground and yelled, "You have to suck out the poison before I die. You have to suck the poison out of my butt cheek!"

Skeeter pointed at where the snake had bitten him. Tick ran over and got down on his knees and started sucking on Skeeter's sweaty, stinky, dirty behind. After a few failed attempts to suck out the poison, Tick looked closer for the bite mark but couldn't find one.

"You dumb hick. You had me suckin' your butt cheek, and there ain't even no bite," Tick fumed.

He went over with a shovel to take care of the snake. He lifted the shovel to strike the venom-filled reptile, but the fake snake fell over. He picked it up. CARL was written on the bottom of the fake rubber snake. He threw the prank snake as far as he could into the forest and fell to the ground in fear. That was my signal to start singing in the spookiest voice I could muster:

Oh, Phantom of the woods, tell me your tale,
Of ancient secrets and nights so pale.
Lost in the mist, your presence is near,
Losing you is my ultimate fear.

Through tangled vines and whispers of trees,
The Phantom wanders, a silent breeze.
Eyes like stars, piercing through the night,
I can not seem to win this fight.

Though I may fear the dark's embrace,
The Phantom beckons in this place.
But in its realm, there's solace found,
A sanctuary where peace resounds.

Jack sang the same song, but just a few notes behind me to make it sound like an echo coming from two different directions. It was pretty terrifying, to be completely fair. The hairs on my arms stood up, and I was the one singing!

"That's Crazy Carl's song! He's haunting us. After all these years, he's getting us back for how we treated him!" Tick said as he ran to his bed to hide under his moldy blanket.

Skeeter was still in the fetal position, trying to recover from fear. He crawled over to his bed and joined his brother under the covers. They held onto each other, shaking in fear. I rolled over, holding my hand over my mouth so they wouldn't hear me belly laughing at their pitiful cuddling sight.

One of them grabbed the bottle of whiskey that they kept near their bed, and they both took a giant swig to take care of their nerves. Little did they know I had crushed up Carl's sleeping pills and put them in their whiskey bottle. It wasn't long before they were snoring away, holding onto one another in their sleep. Tick was sucking his right thumb like a little baby.

At this point, the sun had begun to shine. Jack slowly walked back to join me. We laughed and laughed.

"Did you see Skeeter's face when he ate the deer poop?" laughed Jack.

"Did you see ol' Tick sucking on Skeeter's butt cheek?" I laughed out loud.

"The song scared the heebie jeebies out of them! Oh, I wish Carl could have seen that!" Jack boasted.

We replayed the whole thing over and over, each time pointing out something funnier than the last. We laughed so hard that our faces hurt. Boy, was that fun, but we were only getting started.

It was time to prepare for Phase Two of my plan. This phase would take all day to prepare. Luckily, the Creedy brothers were in a deep, deep sleep. Every once in a while, one of them would mumble something about Carl. It made me happy to know that Carl was taking care of them in their dreamland.

We prepped for Phase Two for most of the day. Pranking is hard work when you do it right. We finished our prank preparation by putting dog food all over Tick and Skeeter's blanket. We had high hopes that the dog food would attract the right guests....

Chapter 30

Phase Two

The sun set over the Eerie Hollow woods, and a deep fog crept in. The Creedy brothers had slept the whole day away and were about to get a rude awakening. Jack and I hid in our predetermined positions. Tonight was going to be good... real good.

I looked at the sleeping Creedy brothers from my hiding spot. I grinned as my hopes had turned into reality. The dog food was too much of a temptation for the night bandits. A family of masked raccoons was having dinner on top of Skeeter and Tick Creedy. One of the braver raccoons began to play with Tick's long, greasy hair with his black paws.

"Momma? Let me sleep a little longer. I don't wanna get up," moaned Tick in his sleep.

Another mischievous raccoon reached down and licked Skeeter's lips.

"Bertha, my love? Is that you? Did you come back after all these years? Oh, I missed your juicy lips," groaned Skeeter.

He reached up, grabbed the raccoon's head, and gave it a giant, wet kiss.

The raccoon did not take kindly to being kissed and slapped Skeeter across the face.

"It is you, Bertha, ain't it!" smiled Skeeter as he slowly opened his eyes.

Skeeter's smile slowly faded as he began to recognize the masked creature that had been so affectionate.

"AHHHHHHHHHHHH!!!!!" Skeeter screamed.

His scream woke Tick, who opened his eyes to a raccoon sitting on his face.

"AHHHHHHHHHHHH!!!!!" Tick screamed.

The raccoons began to panic. They clawed, jumped, and bit their way out of the grasp of the angry, confused Creedy brothers. Tick and Skeeter stood up quickly, slapping at their bodies. They looked at each other in a panic.

I blew into my harmonica at that very moment. I needed to remind them that it was Carl haunting them.

"Crazy Carl! Leave us alone, ya hear me. Leave us alone!" Skeeter belted at the top of his lungs.

I pulled the pin on a stink bomb and tossed it in their direction. It was too dark to see what hit the ground near them. Tick started to sniff the air. He looked at Skeeter with disgust.

"Skeeter, oh boy, ya stink like rotten eggs," blamed Tick.

"It ain't me, it's you! You stink like maggot-infested trash!" retorted Skeeter.

They started to get into a fight. Skeeter pulled Tick's long, gray hair. Tick stuck two fingers up Skeeter's giant nostrils. They wrestled as they said all sorts of naughty words to each other. That's when I lit the long fuse for the firecrackers I had tucked near their makeshift tent. I watched with anticipation as the flame ran from my hiding position down to the firecrackers.

The flame finally hit the hundreds of firecrackers that I had tied together. Pop! Bang! Crack! It sounded like a war of machine guns. Skeeter and Tick ran around in circles like chickens with their heads cut off. They were crying and begging for mercy! That's when they ran into the tripwire....

Chapter 31

Broken Creedy

We were especially proud of this prank because it was the prank that Carl did to us over thirty years after his disappearance. We had to use a "Carl Original" on the Creedy brothers. The tripwire pulled the pin from Carl's net-holding device. The net landed perfectly, covering both Skeeter and Tick completely. The weight of the net brought the old men crashing to the ground together. They struggled to get out of the net's grasp, but the more they struggled, the louder the bells got. That's when Skeeter noticed the Black Widow spiders.

"Black Widows! Get them off! Get them off of me!" cried Skeeter Creedy.

He slapped, punched, kicked, and even headbutted, trying to kill the black eight-legged creatures with red hourglasses on their bellies. Tick did the same thing. Those poor plastic spiders sure took a beating!

Finally, after much thrashing and swearing, Skeeter and Tick freed themselves from the net of spiders and bells. Then, I threw a few smoke bombs into the camp. A deep smoke filled the whole campsite. Skeeter and Tick coughed as they screamed in fear. I signaled Jack for our grand finale....

He pulled on a rope, lifting a skeleton ten feet in the air. It was dressed in a brown trapper hat, red plaid flannel shirt, blue jean overalls, and red wool socks. The smoke bomb created the perfect, scary scene. A lantern dangled from the skeleton's bony fingers, shining light on Crazy Carl's white skull. He held a harmonica near his mouth.

Skeeter and Tick lost their minds at the sight of Crazy Carl's skeleton floating in the air. They grabbed their .270 rifles and took aim at Carl's floating skeleton. They pulled their triggers expecting to take Crazy Carl out, but instead, pink glitter shot out of the end of their guns! While they slept the day away, we had replaced their actual ammo with the fake .270 cartridges that were in Carl's box of tricks.

"Oh, that's classic," I whispered to myself, nodding in perfect approval of Carl's prank.

The looks on the Creedy boys' faces when the wind blew the pink glitter onto their sweaty bodies was priceless! They were covered head to toe in pretty pink sparkles!

Then I blew into my harmonica, and Jack and I sang Carl's song together:

Oh, Phantom of the woods, tell me your tale,
Of ancient secrets and nights so pale.
Lost in the mist, your presence is near,
Losing you is my ultimate fear.

Through tangled vines and whispers of trees,
The Phantom wanders, a silent breeze.
Eyes like stars, piercing through the night,
I can not seem to win this fight.

Though I may fear the dark's embrace,
The Phantom beckons in this place.
But in its realm, there's solace found,
A sanctuary where peace resounds.

Skeeter and Tick were completely frozen with fear. It was beautiful. Absolutely beautiful.

After the song, while the Creedy brothers were frozen in fear, I whispered sternly in my most ghostly voice, "Never step foot in my forest again, or I will haunt you until your last filthy breath!"

That did it. We broke the Creedy brothers. They fell down to the ground, crying, moaning, and begging for forgiveness.

"Carl! We're sorry for not believing you all those years ago about the Phantom Buck. We're sorry for bullying you. We're sorry for poaching in your woods. We will never come back!" Skeeter and Tick cried loudly.

I nodded my head, and Jack nodded in return. We had accomplished our task of ridding the woods of these menaces. I only had one word left for them. I shouted it with ghostly authority.

"Leave!"

They hopped up and ran to their truck, stumbling and bumbling. They started the engine and took off as if they had seen a ghost... because they had!

As the truck drove off, the non-stop sound of a harmonica chased them out of the woods. Jack and I had zip-tied a harmonica to the bottom of their truck....

Chapter 32

Freezing

Jack and I walked back to our camp with our heads held high. We had just put together maybe the greatest series of pranks since the beginning of time. Carl would have been very, very proud of us. I was thankful that the Creedy poachers had learned their lesson and wouldn't be making a mockery of hunting ever again.

Now, it was time to get back to business. There was still a giant Phantom Buck out there calling my name. The next morning, we'd be out there looking for him, but for now, all I could think of was getting some good sleep. We were out as soon as our heads hit our pillows that night.

After a tremendously restful sleep, I woke up. It was still very dark, and Jack was still sleeping. He was moaning and looked like he was having a pretty bad dream. His legs appeared to be trying to run away from something. I tried not to wake him. I got dressed quietly and unzipped the tent. I walked out into the darkness. The frozen grass crunched under my boots.

The early morning air was freezing. I pulled out the map I had copied and studied it under the light of my flashlight. The light shook side to side on the map because I was shivering so badly. I noticed that on the map, there was an X marking the place where we happened to be camped. I wondered if that meant Carl's name was carved into a tree somewhere nearby.

I decided to investigate. I grabbed my flashlight and walked around the area. I shined my light on the bigger trees to see if they, by chance, had the name CARL carved into them. I didn't have much luck. So many trees surrounded our camp that it was impossible to find the one Carl might have carved his name into. I headed back to camp.

Suddenly, I saw white eyes glowing in the moonlight about sixty yards ahead of me. I gulped. At first, I couldn't tell what I saw, but then the Phantom Buck stepped into an opening. He stared right at me.

He moved his head from side to side, showing me his massive, bone-white antlers. They were the most enormous antlers I had ever seen on a deer. They were wide and thick. They made Jack's trophy buck look like a little spike.

I stared until the freezing night air made me close my eyes. When I opened them, he was gone. I shook my head. He really was a phantom.

I walked over to where he stood. I shined my light on the tree next to where I had seen the Phantom. Sure enough, the letters CARL were carved into the tree. My eyes widened as I realized what the Xs stood for on Carl's map. The Xs had to be where Carl had seen the Phantom. After each Phantom encounter, Carl must have carved his name into the nearest tree!

I felt like history was repeating itself. I had now seen the Phantom in two of the exact same places that Carl had! I ran over to the tent and woke Jack up by violently shaking his shoulders.

"Jack, Jack! I saw the Phantom Buck again. The Xs are where Carl saw the Phantom all those years ago. His name was carved into the tree right where I saw the Phantom standing!" I explained loudly.

Jack rubbed his eyes and slapped his cheeks to wake himself up. He blinked repeatedly and then got up and dressed. He didn't really seem to believe me, so I took him to the tree. His eyes got big as he nodded his head.

"Maybe you're right. This can't be a coincidence. But why is the Phantom Buck only showing himself to you?" Jack stated.

"I keep thinking about the curse that Carl put on the town. He said he would haunt the town until he brought the Phantom Buck home with him, right? Maybe he cursed the Phantom Buck at the same time. You know, like this poor buck has not been able to die for thirty-five years? Maybe I'm meant to end the curse for the town AND the Phantom Buck. Maybe since I'm a relative of Carl's, I could harvest the Phantom when no one else could. Then bring the Phantom back to Eerie Hollow and break the curse for everyone!" I reasoned.

"I guess that theory would explain why the Phantom Buck keeps showing himself to just you," reasoned Jack.

We went back to the tent and got our gear and rifles. We studied the map together. The Xs were in a straight line leading deeper into the Eerie Hollow woods. We also noticed another tree stand marked on the map near the last X. I thought it made sense to go check it out. I mean, the first tree stand proved to be pretty successful for Jack.

We tried to make our way to the tree stand in the darkness. We knew we had already camped for two nights, and Mom was expecting us back before she went to bed that night. We would have to hurry to get to this stand before light, hunt all day, and then run home to make our curfew once the sun went down. It would be tough to do, but we would make it happen.

As we walked, I felt the air change. It was definitely getting colder. My hands began to freeze, but I hadn't brought gloves to keep them warm. I put my left wrist up to my face and bit my thin jacket sleeve. I slid my hand inside my sleeve, hoping to warm it up. The wind started to blow hard. The trees began to sway back and forth. An eerie creaking noise came from the trees as they bent in the wind. I wiped my nose with my jacket sleeve. The snot from my nose immediately froze on my sleeve.

Part of me wanted to quit and go home. I thought about my warm, king-sized bed. I imagined myself wrapped up in my warm blanket with a cup of hot chocolate. That would be so delightful, but I must admit that an undeniable part of me told me to push on. I had to harvest the Phantom Buck. I had to....

Sunrise came a lot faster than I thought it would. We had been walking for hours in as straight of a line as we could to get to the stand. It was taking a lot longer to get there than we had predicted. I looked in the sky and saw dark gray clouds. The wind fiercely howled.

"I think we might just get stuck in a blizzard," Jack said in a worried tone as he watched the dark gray clouds rolling in.

"We have come too far to turn back. Let's keep pushing forward," I begged.

"I really don't think that is a good idea. We should go home while we still can. Our parents are going to worry about us, and if it snows, it will make running home before your mom goes to bed impossible," pleaded Jack.

Just then, the sound of a harmonica traveled in the wind. Our eyes got big. It had to mean something. It seemed like Carl was calling to me to find him. I just felt it in my heart. We couldn't stop.

The wind blew harder and harder. The dark clouds threatened to dump heavy snow. I pulled out the map and studied it with Jack. From what we could tell, we had to be close to the tree stand. We had to be.

We looked up in the trees, searching for the stand. I just knew we would find another giant stand like the Rifle Tower, but we didn't see a thing. We walked further and further into the woods. We dropped down into a dark hollow. It was strange. It was nearly ten in the morning now, but down in this particular hollow, it was almost dark.

The wind ripped across my body. My face was freezing. My feet were freezing. My hands were freezing. My everything was freezing. The wind made my eyes tear up, and the tears froze on my cheeks. I closed my eyes for a few moments, trying to gather my thoughts.

Suddenly, I felt something staring at me in the distance. I opened my eyes in the direction of the eerie sensation. Standing on the top of a small ridge was the Phantom Buck. He turned and vanished from my view.

Of course, Jack didn't see him this time either. I started to wonder if I was crazy. Maybe I had been making it up in my mind. Maybe there was no Phantom Buck. Maybe I was just seeing things because I wanted to see them.

My body was exhausted and cold. I had not dressed for this type of weather. I just wanted to collapse, but I had to push forward. The wind continued to get stronger, and now snowflakes were falling. I was scared we would get stuck in a blizzard, because of my hardheadedness. I should have listened to Jack and just gone home.

It wasn't surprising when we found CARL carved into the tree where I saw the Phantom Buck standing. I looked at the map and found the last X. Now, we knew exactly where we were on the map. The tree stand was close. We both searched the trees for a stand. Then I heard Jack laugh.

I looked in his direction. He pointed up towards a tall pine tree. A single board had been placed about twenty feet up between two thick branches. The trunk had grown around the board, but you could still see the ends of it. The ancient pine tree had almost entirely swallowed the small makeshift treestand.

"I don't think Carl spent too much time building this stand. It's nothing like the Rifle Tower. It makes sense, though. We are miles and miles away from home. It would have been really tough to bring building supplies out this far," Jack reasoned.

My heart sank. I pulled out the map. A snowflake fell onto it, then another, and another. The clouds were finally letting go. The wind howled fiercely. The snow flew completely sideways. The blizzard had begun. We were so far from home now. There was nowhere to escape this deadly weather. It got darker and darker....

Chapter 33

Near Death

We sat for hours at the base of the thick pine tree where Carl had carved his name all those years ago. We huddled closely to one another, trying to keep warm. It wasn't working. We were honest-to-goodness freezing to death. The wind swirled angrily as it beat against our bodies relentlessly. There was nowhere to go to shield ourselves from the deadly combination of wind and wet snow. We began to shake uncontrollably. Our situation had become dire. We were no longer hunting. We were merely surviving a life-or-death situation.

I looked down at where my feet should have been. The snow had covered my boots completely. It had already snowed at least a foot with no signs of the blizzard slowing down. I didn't know what to do. There was nowhere to go. There was no shelter to protect us. Soon, we would be completely covered in cold, wet snow.

"Jack, I'm scared. I don't know if we will survive this," I confessed in a quiet whisper.

My teeth chattered loudly. I felt tired and weak. I could feel life slipping out of my frozen body. Jack lifted his head and looked me in the eyes. His light blue eyes, normally filled with so much life, were now dim. He put his head down into his palms.

"I'm scared, too," Jack admitted.

He looked back up at me. Tears welled up in his eyes. He gulped and opened his mouth to speak, but no words came. He closed his eyes and sighed.

"Your mom was right. I have bad nightmares... I have them every night. Every night, that psycho grizzly attacks me in my sleep. I have been too ashamed to talk to you about it. I wanted to look brave, but I am so scared to go to sleep every night knowing I have to face that evil bear in my dreams... I don't know why I am telling you this now. Maybe it's because we'll probably freeze to death, but I wanted to let you know what I have been going through for years now. "

I felt sympathy and compassion swell in my chest. It was a brave thing for a twelve-year-old boy to admit that he lived in that kind of continuous fear. I reached over and hugged my cousin. I felt warm inside for the first time all day. There was no judgment in my heart, just pride in the friendship that we had forged.

"Jack, we are going to survive this blizzard. Then someday, when you're ready, you're going to hunt that evil bear and put an end to his reign of terror. Then, the nightmares will stop. I know they will."

"Do you really think the nightmares would stop?" Jack asked sincerely.

"I'm sure of it," my voice trailed off as the sound of a harmonica interrupted our heart-to-heart conversation.

The words to Carl's song began to play over and over in my mind. For some reason, the words brought warmth to my heart and body. I began to sing Carl's song out loud. Jack didn't seem to mind. He even jumped in, and we sang the last verse together.

Though I may fear the dark's embrace,
The Phantom beckons in this place.
But in its realm, there's solace found,
A sanctuary, where peace resounds.

I thought for a moment and realized that Carl had been scared, too. He confessed it in his song. I looked around. Darkness covered the hollow where we sat. I thought about the Phantom Buck I had seen on this very spot before the snow began to fall. I looked up at Carl's name carved into the tree that I leaned my tired, cold body against. Suddenly, a brilliant thought came into my mind out of nowhere.

"Jack! It's dark here! In this hollow, it is abnormally dark!" I shouted.

"Though I may fear the dark's embrace," I whispered the first line of the last verse of Carl's song, emphasizing the word "dark."

"And I saw the Phantom here," I shouted excitedly.

"The Phantom beckons in this place," I smiled as everything started to make sense to me.

"I'm not sure what you are getting at," Jack admitted.

"This is the place. This is what Carl was singing about in that last verse," I explained.

"But in its realm, there is solace found, a sanctuary where peace resounds," I excitedly quoted the last two lines of the song.

My body filled with adrenaline. I stood up, kicked the snow off my boots, and pulled out the map.

"Look here! The bird on the map! It's not a pheasant or a quail. It's a dove! Doves are a symbol of peace!" I shouted excitedly as I put my finger on the dove.

"Get up! We have to find Carl's sanctuary of peace!" I said as I reached down and grabbed Jack's hand to pull him to his feet.

I oriented the map correctly. We were close to where the dove was marked on the map. Together, we took our first steps toward the place where the dove was marked. We took tall steps through the thick, wet snow. Each step was difficult, but now we were filled with hope. The wind howled and pushed against our tired, cold bodies, but we continued to move forward. I put my forearm above my eyes to block the wind.

I looked through the driving snow. My heart leaped when I saw rocks. I had seen these rocks before.

"The cave in the painting," I shouted over the wind, but the wind threw my words back at me.

"The what?" yelled Jack.

"The cave in the painting," I yelled louder over the howling wind as I pointed at the cave's opening.

"The cave is the answer!" I yelled, this time full of excitement.

"You're right! It looks exactly like the painting," exclaimed Jack.

We ran as fast as we could towards the rocks, which was not very fast at all. It's tough to run through deep snow.

Hope filled our hearts as we got closer and closer to our saving grace, but then the sound of a harmonica stopped us in our tracks. My excitement changed to dread in an instant. The haunting sound of the harmonica had come from inside the cave....

Chapter 34

Tight Tunnel

We stood there and stared at the opening of the cave. I gulped. Jack gulped. We looked at each other with deep concern. I felt fear rip through my tired, freezing body.

"Nope. Nope. Nope," Jack said as he turned around to walk back to the base of Carl's tree.

I pulled him back. He looked at me with a very serious face.

"If there is a harmonica sound coming from the cave, I want nothing to do with it," Jack declared through chattering teeth.

"We have no choice. We have to get shelter, or we will freeze to death," I replied.

"If Carl's ghost is hanging out in that cave, I think I'd rather die out here than get scared to death in there," Jack argued.

I reached down, grabbed Jack's freezing hand, and pulled him back towards me. I told him that our parents would kill us if we froze to death out here. He let out a deep sigh. He knew that I was right. Together, we took a brave step towards the cave.

We stopped a few yards in front of the cave and grabbed our rifles off our backs. We readied them as we walked closer to the mouth of the cave. If anything were in there ready to eat us, it would get a mouth full of lead! I was shaking, but it wasn't because I was freezing. It was because I was absolutely terrified.

Jack and I looked at each other. I grabbed my flashlight out of my pack. I probably looked a bit silly with a gun in one hand and a flashlight in the other, but I wasn't too worried about appearances. The opening of the cave was only a couple of feet wide. A giant spider web covered the entire entrance. I used my flashlight to knock it down. We both took a deep breath before slowly bending down to enter the cave.

I shined my light into the darkness. To our relief, the cave was completely empty, but we saw the strangest thing. The whole cave had been painted the same color of white that Carl had used to paint the eyes of The Phantom of Eerie Hollow. There wasn't an inch of the cave that wasn't painted.

The room, if you want to call it that, was tiny. I couldn't even stand up all the way. I'd guess it was only about eight feet in diameter. There weren't any drawings or any words on the walls. No map on the floor like in Carl's lair. Just an empty, tiny room. Jack and I looked at each other with confusion in our eyes.

Then we heard it again. The sound of a harmonica bounced off the walls of the tiny room. It was loud, and it sounded like it was being played right in front of us. It didn't make any sense. We were alone. At least we thought we were....

I turned around in circles, shining my flashlight everywhere.

"Carl's ghost lives here!" Jack gulped.

I sat down on the floor, trembling with fear. I continued to look around with the flashlight, making sure there weren't any ghosts or anything scary waiting to eat us for lunch.

Then, I noticed a dark spot in the back wall of the cave. It looked like it could be a hole! I rushed over to the black void and shined my flashlight into it. It was a creepy-looking tunnel. The tunnel was just big enough for a grown person to squeeze through it if they really wanted to.

"Jack, there is a tunnel over here."

He came over and looked at it with me. He got on his knees next to me. We both looked into the tunnel together with the flashlight. We both had our heads in the entrance to the tunnel when we heard the harmonica sound again. This time, it was really loud. It came from the tunnel!

"Nope, I'm not going in there. I know that's what you're thinking, McKay, but not me. Nope. No way. We found shelter. We can wait out the storm here just fine. There's no reason to go in there," Jack stammered.

My stomach dropped as I thought about going through the tunnel. I've been scared of tight spaces my whole life, and the thought of getting stuck inside a tunnel and being unable to turn around made me want to vomit.

I had to do it, though. I had to find the source of the sound of the harmonica, even if it meant I'd have to face my biggest fear. I closed my eyes briefly and gathered every bit of courage I could muster. I reached into my backpack and pulled out a length of rope. I tied the rope to my right foot and gave Jack the other end of the rope.

"If I get stuck, pull me out! If I make it without dying of a panic attack, you can follow the rope to find me," I explained.

I took a deep breath and put my head into the tunnel. I pushed forward with my feet. I army crawled for a few feet until I felt a giant spider web cover my face. Panic jolted a deafening scream out of my throat. My spirit may have even left my body, but instead of just laying there freaking out, I power crawled through the spider web as fast as I could.

My body started trembling. I began to sweat... a lot. I had to keep moving forward, though. I tried to ignore the giant spider I felt crawling on my neck. I couldn't reach it with my hands, though. There wasn't enough room in the tunnel. The edges of the tunnel pushed on the sides of my body. I wanted to give in to the overwhelming feeling I had to faint, but I knew I couldn't.

I squinted, took a deep breath, and continued to crawl into the tunnel's depths.

At this point, there was no returning to the white room. I had gone too far. My heart was beating a thousand beats per second. I sang Carl's song to try to calm my heart down. It helped. It felt like Carl was there with me. Helping me. Then, suddenly, the tunnel dropped downwards. I began sliding downhill on the super smooth rock floor as if on a metal slide at a park. I slid until the tunnel spit me out into an open space.

I instinctively got up on my knees and then stood up. I reached for the spider on my neck and squashed it. I slapped at my face to remove the spider web. Once I got the web off my face, I took a deep breath and sighed with deep relief.

I had survived the long, tight, creepy tunnel! I had conquered one of my biggest fears. Excitement filled my chest. I was really, really proud of myself. I smiled one of the biggest smiles of my lifetime. My breathing started to slow, and my heart calmed down. I shined my flashlight around me. My jaw dropped when I realized what I was seeing....

Chapter 35

Carl's Masterpiece

I stood in silence for a few moments as I shined my flashlight into the spacious cavern. The ceiling had been painted like the Sistine Chapel. A beautiful mural filled the entire ceiling of the cavern. It was a painting of Great Grandpa Willie sitting next to the pond on a bench with Carl and Cliff. They held each other's hands. It had been painted so that you could see the love those three men had for each other. A tear came to my eye.

The walls were painted too. They were covered with memories of Carl's life. One of the paintings was of Carl and Cliff sitting in the Rifle Tower. They held their rifles with big smiles on their faces. Their bright green eyes lit up with excitement as a big buck showed himself in the meadow. The same meadow where Jack had shot his giant buck when my gun had misfired.

Another painting on the wall made me laugh out loud. Carl sat at a table in an old diner with two kids. Carl and the kids were holding their bellies with smiles full of laughter. Across the table from them was an older gentleman with gray bushy eyebrows. It looked like he had just taken a drink from his coffee mug. His face squinted as orange juice spewed out of his mouth.

I smiled a giant, toothy smile at seeing a painting that showed Grandpa Cliff tossing my toddler dad in the air. Carl had his hands reached out and was waiting to catch him. Dad had the funniest smile as he flew through the air, waiting for his uncle to catch him.

I continued to smile as my light made its way around the room. Every inch of this cavern was painted with a memory. Then, suddenly, the cold metal flashlight slipped from the grasp of my sweaty fingers. A beam of light ricocheted off the cave walls as the flashlight rolled on the rocky cave floor. It finally came to a stop at the far end of the cavern.

I walked over to where the flashlight lay motionless. As I bent over to pick it up, I felt my face rub against something strange. It felt like the fabric of a pair of jeans. I gulped as I grabbed the flashlight off the floor. I shined it on the ground in front of me. My eyes focused on a pair of red wool socks. I slowly lifted the light to see a pair of jean overalls. Then I saw a red plaid flannel shirt. I stood slightly and found myself face to face with a white skull covered in a brown trapper hat!

I fell over backwards, scared out of my mind. I kicked my feet to try to get away. I kept my light fixed on the skeleton. Suddenly, I realized who it was that I was looking at. I stopped kicking and stood up slowly.

"Carl?" I whispered to the skeleton sitting on a wooden bench.

"It's you, isn't it?" I whispered.

All the fear that was still in my body left. I felt peaceful in Carl's presence. I should have been scared to death standing before a real-life skeleton, but now I wasn't scared at all. I knelt down in front of Carl. My heart slowed down. I began to cry tears of joy.

"Carl, I found you. I found you. You need to know that your dad loved you so much. Cliff still loves you. You have been missed. It's time to go home. I'll take you home, I promise."

We were in such a beautiful, sacred place—a sanctuary where peace resounds. I looked at the beautiful paintings again. I smiled, knowing Carl died with these memories right in front of him. In that way, I knew he wasn't alone when the end finally came.

I looked at his bony fingers and saw that he was still holding his infamous harmonica. I looked closely at the harmonica. It was fancy! It was silver and had neat engravings all over it. Just then, a breeze came from a hole in the cavern right behind him. It blew directly through the harmonica. The harmonica played a tune. But this time, instead of making a creepy sound, the music sounded happy.

"McKay! What's going on? Did you find whatever is making that harmonica noise?" yelled Jack through the tunnel.

"Jack, you're going to want to see this," I hollered back.

"Uggghhh, I knew you were going to say that," he replied.

"Tie the rope to something. We'll need to use it to get out," I yelled through the tunnel.

I heard Jack breathe in and out, trying to gain the courage to enter the tunnel. It was amazing how well the tunnel carried sound. I could hear every tiny sound that he made. I waited patiently as he worked his way through the tunnel. He slid down the end of the tunnel and landed at my feet.

"You're welcome," I said.

"What the heck for?" replied Jack as he breathed deeply in and out.

"For cleaning out all of the spiderwebs with my face," I retorted.

He nodded in appreciation as I helped him get to his feet. I looked him in the eyes with a giant smile on my face.

"Are you ready for this?" I asked.

"It better be good. I didn't crawl through that tunnel just to see some rocks," he said with a bit of sarcasm in his voice.

"I promise it won't disappoint," I replied, slowly pointing the light to the ceiling.

I watched Jack's eyes light up. He stared at the painting for a few moments in silence. Then, I slowly shined the light on the walls. His jaw dropped to the floor as each scene on the wall lit up for him to see.

"I've never seen anything like this. This cavern could be an art museum. Carl's paintings are beyond amazing," Jack stated.

"Just wait until you see this...."

I turned my flashlight off and let the darkness take over the room.

"McKay, quit messing around. Turn the light back on," begged Jack.

"If you say so," I replied.

I aimed my flashlight at Carl and turned it on. Jack jumped at least three feet in the air at the sight of the skeleton. He screamed a high-pitched scream.

"Oh, calm down. Carl isn't that scary," I smirked.

"Carl? Wait! What? You found Carl!" Jack exclaimed as he gave me a big hug.

"I did," I said proudly as I pointed to the harmonica in Carl's hand.

"That's the harmonica that has been haunting Eerie Hollow for the past thirty-five years. Whenever the wind blows just right, it plays a few notes that carry through the tunnel we just came through. Then, the sound gets louder as it leaves through the opening of the white room. You know, kind of like how a trumpet works. I'm guessing that's why the sound carried such a long distance all the way back to town," I explained.

As if on cue, the wind blew into the cavern, making the harmonica play a few notes. We both smiled. We had solved the mystery together.

It was cold in the cavern but definitely warmer than outside. Carl had made a small fire pit in front of his wooden bench. I pictured Carl playing his harmonica as he watched the fire dance on the paintings on the walls.

I noticed that in the corner, there were still a few sticks of neatly stacked dry wood. There was some kindling as well. Carl must have brought firewood every time he came to the cave. I guess he didn't get a chance to use all the wood before he passed away.

Jack pulled out his True Hunter flint and steel and some dryer lint from his backpack. He scraped the steel across the flint, and sparks showered onto the dryer lint. In no time, flames were dancing on the dry logs. We watched as the smoke went out through the small hole in the wall that acted like a chimney. It was a perfect system. It felt so incredibly good to be warm again.

As we watched the light of the fire dance on Carl's paintings, we decided to catch Carl up on everything that had happened on our adventure. We told him all about scaring the stink off the Creedy brothers. He seemed to smile when we told him about each prank. I told him about the Phantom Buck and that he still lived. I told Carl that his twin was my Grandpa Cliff. I shared how badly my Grandpa Cliff took his disappearance. I told him we found his secret lair behind his painting of The Phantom of Eerie Hollow. We shared how impressed we were by his creativity. It was wonderful. Really wonderful.

We slept in the cavern near the fire until the storm finally passed the next morning. We knew we needed to get home. We could only imagine how worried our parents must have been when we didn't come home the night before the storm. I had made a promise to my mom and broke it willingly before the storm had even started. We should have gone back home when Jack suggested it.

I looked at the True Hunter engraving on the handle of the flint that was lying on the floor. I decided that a True Hunter always keeps his promises and doesn't leave people to worry about them while they are out in the woods. I made a promise to myself never to break a promise ever again.

Jack and I discussed it and figured out a way to bring Carl home. We carefully wrapped Carl's skeleton in a blue tarp that Carl had left in the cavern. It was next to some of his painting supplies that he had used to paint the cavern. We tied the rope that led to the white room around the tarp.

Jack followed the rope back to the white room. I followed right after him. Then we both pulled on the rope carefully and dragged Carl to the room he had painted white thirty-five years ago. Thankfully, we got him through the tunnel without damaging his skeleton. We grabbed our guns and stuck our heads out of the cave entrance. The snow was so deep it almost closed off the entrance.

We decided that the only way to get Carl home was to build a sled and pull him. We went to work immediately. We tied some branches together in the shape of a rectangle. We wrapped the blue tarp around the branches and tied a rope to the front. We laid Carl in the center of the tarp. We both pulled, and luckily, the sled slid on top of the fresh snow. We smiled and nodded with satisfaction. We were pretty proud of our ingenuity.

Chapter 36

Sledding Skeleton

We made our way through the dark hollow. Pulling Carl up the last steep hill out of the darkness was really hard. When we crested the top of the hollow, I watched as the light of the sun hit Carl's face for the first time in thirty-five years. It felt like an accomplishment to bring Carl into the light. He had been in the dark for far too long.

Jack and I decided to take a break. We sat in the soft, deep snow. I pulled out the map to understand how far we were from home. It was quite depressing how far away we still were. My heart hurt for my parents. I was sure they were panicking that their boy hadn't come home before the storm hit. I sighed. This would be a very long day for me and them.

It was still early in the morning, though. Jack and I were hopeful that we would make it home before dark. I looked at the scenery around us. Everything was white.

Sunlight glimmered on the fresh snow as far as our eyes could see. The woods looked completely different than they did the day before. The trees were covered in white snow that bent the limbs downward with its weight.

I looked around and noticed a ton of damage caused by the storm. The heavy snow had broken giant limbs off of ancient trees. The wind had blown some trees down. The poor trees had their roots ripped right out of the ground. This blizzard was no joke, that's for sure. I was so thankful we had found Carl's cavern to keep us safe from the worst of the blizzard. I don't know if we would have survived if Carl's map didn't lead us to the cave.

We sat on the top of a big hill. I looked down below us. There was a clear pathway all the way to the bottom, not even a single tree. I began to grin as a fun idea popped into my head.

"Tell me, Jack. Have you ever gone sledding with a skeleton before?" I asked.

My grin grew larger as I looked at Jack. My eyebrows raised higher with each passing moment. Jack began to nod and returned my look with a mischievous grin of his own.

"You know, I don't believe I ever have, but I do think Carl could use a little fun in his afterlife," Jack joked.

We readied the sled and giggled, anticipating the epic ride we could brag about to our own kids someday.

I mean, how many kids have ever sledded down a monster hill with a skeleton?

I hopped in front, and Carl sat quietly behind me. Jack grabbed onto the back of the sled and started to push. He ran as fast as he could. The sled began to slide down the steep hill. Jack hopped on, and we immediately picked up some major speed. We hit a small bump and bounced into the air for a moment.

"Yippee!" I yelled.

"Woohoo!" Jack shouted at the top of his lungs.

I looked down at the bottom of the hill and saw a perfect place to jump the sled. There was no way that I was going to let the opportunity to hit a jump with a skeleton on my sled pass me by. I pointed at the jump and yelled back to Jack to lean to the right. He smiled big and leaned with me. Our homemade sled veered to the right perfectly towards our intended target. We gained speed. A lot of speed. Maybe too much speed. Snow sprayed up into my eyes. I couldn't see anything.

I braced myself for the epic jump I was sure we were about to hit. Suddenly, I felt the sled turn upward, and we went completely airborne. We flew through the air like eagles. It was exhilarating! Jack and I hooped and hollered as we soared. Then, our sled turned downward as we lost our upward momentum. The ground came quickly. Our makeshift sled hit the ground nose first. It flipped, tossing Jack, Carl, and me through the air. I hit the snow face first with a thud. Carl's skeleton landed on top of me.

I pulled my head out of the snow. My face looked like a snowman! All I needed was a carrot for my nose. I knocked the snow off of my face. I felt Carl's bony hand lying on my shoulder. I turned to look at Carl. He, too, looked like a snowman. I brushed the snow off of his skull. It was a good thing he was wearing his trapper hat to keep him warm. It looked to me like Carl was smiling big time.

"Carl! That... was... awesome..." I shouted.

I grabbed his hand on my shoulder to move it, but I noticed that his pointer finger was extended. It looked like he was pointing at something in front of us. I slowly turned my head to look in the direction he pointed....

Chapter 37

Two Legends

I rubbed my eyes and blinked over and over. I couldn't believe what I was seeing. The Phantom of Eerie Hollow stood broadside in a clearing not more than a hundred yards in front of us. His bright white eyes seemed to stare right through me. It felt like he was looking right at Carl. His double drop tine antlers glimmered in the sunshine. My heart began to leap out of my chest. Thankfully, I wasn't the only one who saw him this time.

"McKay! Is that the Phantom Buck?" whispered Jack.

I looked in the direction of the voice and saw Jack kneeling about ten feet to my left. I nodded slowly to let him know that this was, in fact, The Phantom of Eerie Hollow.

"McKay! The curse! You have to break the curse! Carl can't come home without that buck!" Jack whispered sharply.

He was right. Carl had to bring the Phantom Buck home with him. Now was my chance to break the curse. I looked around for my rifle, but it was nowhere to be seen. I began to panic. I looked at Jack for help. He realized that I didn't have my rifle. Luckily, his rifle was still on his back. He slowly grabbed it. He put the rifle butt into his shoulder and took aim. He hesitated before pulling the bolt back to load a bullet....

"Shoot him! Do it now before he vanishes," I whispered.

Jack pulled his eye away from the scope and looked at me for a moment. He lowered the rifle. He shook his head.

"McKay, it has to be you."

Then Jack did the craziest thing. He put his hand on the butt of his rifle, and he tossed the gun in the air towards me. I watched the rifle fly in slow motion. My mind raced with what I would have to do next. I had to be quick and silent, or the Phantom would disappear again. Maybe even disappear forever.

I reached out and snatched the rifle out of the air. In one smooth motion, I put the butt of the gun into my shoulder, pulled the bolt back to load a bullet, and put my finger on the trigger. I looked down the scope. I fully expected the Phantom Buck to have disappeared, but the Phantom did not move a muscle this time. It was as if he had lived for this moment, too.

I put the crosshairs behind his muscular shoulder. I breathed in deeply and let my breath out slowly. The

Phantom of Eerie Hollow stood there in all of his magnificent glory. He seemed to take a deep breath with me. I watched as he closed his eyes and let out his final breath. The cold winter air changed his breath into a cloud of pure white mist.

I pulled the trigger and watched as the Phantom Buck fell to the ground. It was a moment that would be etched into my memory forever. I stood up and looked at Carl. Carl's jaw had dropped. He looked super excited. I reached down and picked his skeleton up. I carried Carl over to The Phantom of Eerie Hollow and sat him down next to his ghostly companion.

I knelt beside the pair and took in the special moment with them. I put Carl's hand in mine and whispered into the Phantom's ear.

"Thank you for bringing me to Carl. Thank you for giving your life. Now, the two of you can finally rest in peace."

Jack came over quietly and put his hand on my shoulder. Together, we had done it. Together, we had brought these two legends to this special moment. Carl and his buck had both played the role of The Phantom of Eerie Hollow for far too long.

Jack knelt down and took a deep look into the Phantom's white eyes.

"McKay, look at his eyes. Do you see how the whiteness covers his pupil? He was blind. The Phantom Buck was blind this whole time. I bet you his other senses were much more keen because of that. No wonder no one could ever harvest him," explained Jack.

I nodded my head slowly. It made sense. Not even poachers with a spotlight could get him. I reached over and grabbed his antlers. I had never seen such a large set of antlers in my life. I put my hands on each of his drop tines. He looked exactly like Carl's painting. I was so excited to bring Carl and his Phantom Buck home together at last.

Jack looked into the Phantom's mouth and studied his teeth. Jack explained that you can figure out how old a buck is by how his molars have been worn down. A strange look came over Jack's face.

"McKay, this buck is only five and a half years old," he explained.

"How is that possible?" I asked.

"Maybe you were right. Maybe the Phantom was cursed, too. Maybe he stopped aging when Carl died. The Phantom Buck must have known you had to be the ONE to help break the curse. That's why he led you to Carl," Jack said as he shrugged his shoulders.

I felt the misfired cartridge in my pocket.

"Maybe it was my destiny to bring these two to-gether. I guess I really was the ONE," I said, looking back at Jack.

"I think you're right," Jack said as he winked at me.

We both grunted loudly as we lifted the Phantom onto the sled. Carl and the Phantom Buck laid peace-fully together. The two of them were pretty heavy, but

Jack and I were able to pull them. We began the long trip home, and after an hour or so of tramping through the snow, I heard my name being yelled in the distance.

Jack and I pulled the sled as fast as possible towards the yelling. Then Mom, Dad, and Dallas emerged from the trees ahead of us. Mom looked like a track star running through the deep snow to get to us.

"McKay! McKay!" she yelled as she fell upon my chest.

She was crying big crocodile tears. She hugged me and pounded on my chest with her fist.

"You scared me to death. I thought we lost you forever," she wept.

Dallas made it to Jack and gave him a giant bear hug as he lifted Jack off the ground.

"Squirt! I love you, buddy! Don't ever scare me like that again!" he belted.

Dad finally reached me and joined Mom in the hug. We hugged tightly. Tears streamed out of my eyes as I looked in the direction they had come. I blinked over and over when I thought I saw Grandpa Cliff come out of the treeline.

"Is that Grandpa Cliff?" I asked.

"It is. I called him when you didn't come home last night. He didn't hesitate to come back to Eerie Hollow to help us find you," Dad explained.

I pulled away from the hug and looked Mom and Dad in the eyes. They hadn't noticed what we had been hauling in the sled yet, and I wanted to keep it that way until Grandpa Cliff got to us. I waited for a few moments until Grandpa got to me. I gave him a big hug.

"Grandpa Cliff, I found him," I whispered into his ear as we hugged.

He pulled away with a confused look on his face. Then, I stepped to the side and pointed to the home-made tarp sled. Grandpa Cliff fell to his knees when he saw his twin brother's skeleton next to The Phantom of Eerie Hollow.

"Carl? Is that Carl?" Grandpa Cliff said through flowing tears.

"It is," I said solemnly.

Grandpa Cliff knelt next to his twin's skeleton. He carefully held Carl's bony hand and looked back at me.

"How?" he asked.

"The Phantom Buck led us to him," I explained.

At that moment, Grandpa Cliff's demeanor changed. His hardened exterior turned softer. It looked like a significant burden had been lifted from his shoulders.

I looked over at Mom and Dad. They seemed pretty confused about what was going on.

"Hold on a second. Are you telling me that you found Crazy Carl?" Dad asked, completely confused.

"Don't call my twin brother Crazy," Grandpa Cliff said, defending Carl.

"Whoa! Are you saying that Carl is your twin?" Dad asked Grandpa Cliff.

"He is. I haven't spoken his name since I left Eerie Hollow all those years ago. It hurt too much to think about him, but it looks like these boys found him. Let's bring Carl back to town with his Phantom Buck. Let's end this curse nonsense forever," whispered Grandpa Cliff.

Chapter 38

Broken Curse

We all took turns pulling the sled holding Carl and The Phantom of Eerie Hollow. Dallas made it look easier than it really was. I wished I had arms as big as him.

Finally, after a long, long day of hiking through snow, we made it up the last hill near the mansion house. The sun was beginning to set. We stopped at Carl's tree. I looked over at Jack, and he smiled back at me.

"I bet you this was the first place that these two met," I said to Jack as I pointed at the sled.

"I bet you are right. I wish I could have seen Carl's eyes when he first laid eyes on the Phantom Buck," Jack responded thoughtfully.

We all took a break at the mansion house to get food and drinks. Jack and I were absolutely starving. Mom brought out deer stew leftovers from last night's meal that we had missed. We scarfed them down in seconds. It tasted so good after such a long hike through the snow. We licked our plates to get every bit of the yummy goodness. After our stomachs were filled, I looked over at Grandpa Cliff.

"Are you ready to finally end this curse?" I asked.

"I am. I am so ready to end this whole thing," he replied.

Fittingly, it was the last day of The Festival of The Phantom of Eerie Hollow. A thick, eerie fog had rolled into town. The lights of lanterns appeared to float in the streets as actors walked slowly, singing Carl's song. Grandpa Cliff shook his head as if he were in pain.

"I remember that awful night perfectly. I remember the ghostly look in Carl's eyes. I remember the fire burning around him as he cursed us all. I stopped him before he went into the woods and begged him not to go, but he couldn't be swayed. I knew if he went into the woods that night, I would never see him again alive," Grandpa Cliff shared quietly.

The makeshift sled made a scratching sound on the pavement as Jack and I pulled it slowly down Main Street together. One by one, the people in the street began to stare at us. Quiet whisperings filled their mouths. Then I saw the friendly face of Stan Truman. He walked slowly toward us with an indescribable look on his face. When he reached us, he stopped walking. He looked me in the eyes. Then he moved his head to look around me. His eyes fell on the sled. The Phantom Buck was lying in Carl's arms.

"McKay.... You found Carl?" Stan asked carefully.

"Is that the Phantom Buck in his arms?" Stan asked in almost a whisper.

With a sense of victory in my voice, I said, "Carl has fulfilled his promise. He has returned with The Phantom of Eerie Hollow."

"You broke the curse?" Stan mumbled under his breath.

His eyes lit up. A toothy smile filled his entire face.

"You broke the curse!" Stan shouted at the top of his lungs.

He turned and ran onto the stage in the center of town. He grabbed the microphone. He tapped the microphone with his hand to make sure it was on.

"Attention everyone! Attention! I have an announcement to make!" Stan shouted into the microphone.

He motioned for Jack and me to come onto the stage with him. Jack and I looked at each other and nodded. We knew what needed to be done. I looked over at Uncle Dallas.

"Do you think you could lift the sled onto the stage so everyone can see Carl with the Phantom Buck?" I asked.

Uncle Dallas smiled and flexed his giant bicep. His shirt ripped a little bit around his bulging arm. We walked up to the stage, and Uncle Dallas lifted the homemade sled with a Viking-like grunt. Stan smiled enthusiastically as he cleared his throat to speak.

"These two young men have fulfilled their destiny this evening. They have helped Carl keep his oath! Carl has returned to Eerie Hollow with the Phantom Buck in his arms! The curse has officially been broken!" Stan proclaimed proudly.

The crowd erupted in cheers. The moment seemed unreal. We spent hours shaking people's hands and sharing our adventures. Jack and I were treated as heroes. We showed everyone the white eyes of The Phantom of Eerie Hollow. The newspaper interviewed us. They said Carl and the Phantom Buck would be the front-page story. It was all very exciting.

Jack and I stood side by side as The Festival of The Phantom of Eerie Hollow came to an end. I thought about our experience. I knew we had done it together. We had faced our fears and grown very close. I walked over to Stan and whispered a request in his ear. He nodded in agreement. He gave me the microphone. I gulped as I looked out at the giant crowd.

"Umm... I think it would be nice. Umm... If we all sang Carl's song one last time together," I said as I pulled Carl's silver harmonica from my pocket.

I blew into the harmonica, and a few spooky sounds fell on the ears of all in attendance that night. I started to sing, and the entire crowd joined me.

Oh, Phantom of the woods, tell me your tale,
Of ancient secrets and nights so pale.
Lost in the mist, your presence is near,
Losing you is my ultimate fear.

Through tangled vines and whispers of trees,
The Phantom wanders, a silent breeze.
Eyes like stars, piercing through the night,
I can not seem to win this fight.

Though I may fear the dark's embrace,
The Phantom beckons in this place.
But in its realm, there's solace found,
A sanctuary where peace resounds.

It was a special moment. It was a beautiful end to a tragic story. Jack and I stood alone on the stage. My heart was full from the day's events. I looked at Jack and said,

"Jack, we will get the Phantom Buck mounted. Then, you and I will take turns placing his memory in our homes until the day we die. Deal?" I said as I put my hand out.

"Deal!" Jack said as we shook on it.

Chapter 39

Grandpa Cliff Time

We went home that evening with my family. We figured it was time to share everything we had learned about Carl with our parents and Grandpa Cliff. The first thing Jack and I did was show them the painting in Great Grandpa Willie's office. My dad stared at the painting for a few minutes in silence.

"I'm guessing Carl is the guy with the frog?" Dad asked.

"He is. He loved to put frogs on our Dad's shoulders. He was such a playful person. He was always so happy and fun to be around," explained Grandpa Cliff.

I went over to the desk and pressed the secret button. The drawer with the journal popped out of the desk. I grabbed the journal and handed it to Grandpa Cliff.

"I think Great-Grandpa Willie would want you to have this," I said respectfully.

Grandpa Cliff fingered through the pages. His eyes welled up with tears. He closed the journal and traced Willie's name on the cover with his finger.

"I wish I would have come back sooner. I wish I could have said goodbye before Willie passed away. I would give anything to have more time with him," he stated solemnly.

Next, we took the adults to the painting that covered the lair. They were all amazed at how the Phantom Buck I shot looked precisely like the buck in the painting. Jack and I had agreed to show them the lair. We had argued about keeping it a secret for ourselves, but there was just too much history in there to ignore. Jack reached up and got the key out of the brow tine, stuck the key into the cave of the painting, and opened the painting door.

Every adult's jaw hit the floor when they saw Carl's lair. It was fun to see them get so excited over everything Carl had done in there.

"How did you find this place?" Grandpa Cliff asked.

I looked over at Mom. I didn't want to remind her that we had lit firecrackers in the house in her favorite pot and followed the smoke behind the painting, so I just shrugged my shoulders.

"Guess we got lucky?" I said as I shot a look of guilt at Jack.

The next few days were a blur. Grandpa Cliff

and I spent some much-needed Grandpa-Grandson time together. I took him to the Rifle Tower. We sat there in silence for a good half hour. He had tears in his eyes the whole time. I took him to the cave where Jack and I found Carl. When we stepped into the cave opening, he looked around at the white-painted walls. He knelt down and put his hand on his chin.

"McKay, have you noticed Carl's obsession with this white paint?" Grandpa Cliff asked.

"I have. He used it on everything. The eyes of the buck, the antlers, the words to his song, and this cave," I replied.

He nodded, his eyebrows turning downward as if he were in deep thought. Then I showed him the tight tunnel to the place where I had found Carl. He didn't even hesitate. He went straight into it. He was so brave.

As we entered the open cavern, peace fell over both of us. Grandpa Cliff ran his fingers along the paintings. He stopped when he got to the place where Carl had painted the two of them holding hands with their dad, Willie. He put his hand out and held it on Carl's painted hand.

"McKay, thank you for bringing me here. I haven't felt this peaceful in thirty-five years," he whispered solemnly.

Before we left the room, Grandpa Cliff reached down and picked up the paint tray that Carl had left on the cavern floor. Then, we hiked back to Eerie Hollow. When we got there, Grandpa Carl headed straight to the police station. I wasn't sure why we were there, but Grandpa Cliff took some time talking to the Sheriff alone. He left the paints with the Sheriff. Then he put his arm around me, and we walked home together.

A couple of days later, there was a knock on the door. The Sheriff asked to speak with Grandpa Cliff. Dad and I watched together as Grandpa Cliff nodded his head repeatedly as the Sheriff spoke to him. He turned and looked at us.

"I was right," Grandpa Cliff said.

"About what?" I asked.

"My twin brother Carl," he paused for a second as a half smile broke across his face.

He continued, "I read Willie's journal. It said Carl had been having trouble sleeping, joint pain, and stomach pain during the months that he was losing his mind. The journal also reminded me that Carl would chew on the end of his paintbrush when he was in deep thought. McKay showed me all the things Carl had painted in that special white color, which got me thinking. In the past, artists would go crazy because of a certain white paint that had lead in it. The lead gave the white a special brightness that Carl must have thought necessary to paint the Phantom Buck's eyes and antlers. So, I had Carl's white paint tested for lead," he explained.

Then he pointed to the Sheriff standing at the front door.

"The Sheriff just verified my theory. Carl didn't go crazy because of a giant buck. It was lead poisoning. The white paint he used to draw the eyes and antlers of the Phantom Buck poisoned him!"

Grandpa Cliff shook the Sheriff's hand and said goodbye. He walked into the living room and sat on the heavy couch that my dad made me carry when we first moved in. Grandpa Cliff stretched out his arms, took a deep breath, and let the air out slowly.

"Mckay. Do you know what I am feeling right now? Grandpa Cliff asked softly.

I shook my head. I wasn't sure what he was feeling.

"Closure," he said.

"Closure? What do you mean?" I asked.

"I feel like my mind can finally rest because I know what really happened to Carl."

"Oh, ya, I can understand that," I replied.

"I knew Carl didn't go crazy over a buck," Grandpa whispered under his breath, looking relieved.

Chapter 40

The Plan

My whole family sat around the dinner table in the expansive dining room of our beautiful mansion. Jack and Dallas would be returning to Alaska in the morning, so we decided to have one last yummy dinner. Mom made her famous spaghetti with venison from Jack's trophy buck. Grandpa Cliff sat at the head of the table. He had chosen to move back into the mansion and live with us. Everything was wonderful.

Suddenly, there was a knock at the door. I jumped up, ran to the big oak doors, and swung them open. Stan was standing there with a big ol' grin on his face.

"McKay! It's so good to see you again!" expressed Stan.

"Good to see you too, Stan!" I said as I shook his hand properly.

"Your Grandpa Cliff and Dad wouldn't happen to be nearby, would they?" asked Stan.

"Dad! Grandpa! Stan is at the door!" I hollered.

Dad and Grandpa got up from dinner and made their way into the marbled entryway.

"Stan, come on in," Dad said as he motioned for him to enter.

"I will in a moment. First, there is something I need to show you," Stan said.

He turned to the side and put his arm out. An old man with a cane got out of a very expensive-looking, black vehicle. He slowly made his way towards the door. He had his head down, so all I could see was the messy white hair on the top of his head. When he finally made it to the doorway, he looked up. The old man looked around the room slowly. Then, his kind gaze fell upon me. A playful smile emerged from underneath his white, handlebar mustache. His kind eyes sparkled behind his wire-rimmed glasses.

An audible gasp from Grandpa Cliff filled the entryway. I looked up at the painting above the mantle and looked back at the old man. My eyes almost popped out of my head. It was Great- Grandpa Willie! I watched in silence as he walked through the giant oak doors into the mansion home. Dad and Grandpa Cliff stared with their mouths wide open. It was like they were looking at a ghost.

"It appears I have some explaining to do," said Great-Grandpa Willie.

"But... but... but your ashes are in the urn above the fireplace," Grandpa Cliff said in utter confusion like he wasn't convinced that Willie was alive.

Great-Grandpa Willie walked up to the urn and lifted the lid. We all turned away and cringed... But when we looked back, we saw that the stuff inside the urn wasn't gray. It was colorful. Great-Grandpa Willie lifted the urn to his lips and poured the contents into his mouth. He chewed slowly as his eyes lit up with happiness.

"What?" Great-Grandpa Willie asked, his mouth still full. "You don't like M&Ms?"

I laughed out loud. I ran up to him and put my hand out.

"Can I have some?" I asked with a giant grin.

Great-Grandpa Willie poured some of the urn's candy contents into my outstretched hands.

"Ah, McKay, the man of the hour. You figured out the great mystery! I just knew you were the ONE who would bring my family back together," he said with a wink and a glimmer in his eyes.

"Wait. This was all part of your plan?" I asked.

"Well... Yes. It was indeed. It wouldn't be proper to take all the credit, though. Stan here played an important role. He is quite the actor, wouldn't you agree?"

Stan shrugged. Then he bowed like the actor that he truly was.

"I figured that the only way to get my family back together was to solve the mystery behind Carl's disappearance. If you want a mystery solved right, you must involve a couple of twelve-year-olds, right?

I looked over at Jack and nodded. Then, Great-Grandpa Willie gave me a great big bear hug. Dad and Grandpa Cliff joined in on the hug. Excitement filled the room. Then, Great-Grandpa Willie paused momentarily and looked around the mansion house.

"You all wouldn't mind if I moved back in, though, right?"

The End

Chapter 41

Epilogue

You would not believe how things have changed in Eerie Hollow since I said "The End."

The whole town revolved around Crazy Carl's ghost story, right? To the townsfolk, it seemed that Jack and I ruined the town's biggest money-making event. I mean, who would come to a festival about a solved ghost story?

That's where Great-Grandpa Willie came into the picture. This guy didn't get filthy rich by being a dumb dumb. He devised a plan to turn the ghost story into a celebration of Carl's life. Great-Grandpa Willie built a museum on Main Street where Carl's paintings were proudly put on display for all to see. His painting of The Phantom of Eerie Hollow was definitely a crowd-pleaser. Next to the painting hung a replica of the Phantom Buck with his white glowing eyes and enormous antlers matching the painting perfectly.

A replica of the cavern was built in the museum as well. Great-Grandpa Willie built it so everyone could experience the beautiful last paintings of Carl's life. To enter this part of the museum, you had to crawl through a tunnel.

Once you made it through the tunnel, you experience the room the way I experienced it, with only the light of a flashlight. In the corner of the cavern, you find Carl's skeleton sitting on a bench, dressed in a brown trapper hat, a red plaid flannel shirt, filthy jean overalls, and red wool socks. He holds a silver harmonica in his hand. As you can imagine, the museum turned out to be a big hit, and people came to Eerie Hollow year-round to see it for themselves.

In the fall, The Festival of The Phantom of Eerie Hollow continued. Actors dress like Carl and walk the streets with lanterns, singing his song. The ghost story is still told in the woods by the bushy mustache man, but the story doesn't end with Carl cursing the town. It ends with the story of Jack and I finding Carl's skeleton, sledding with him, shooting the Phantom Buck, and bringing Carl home with the Phantom in his arms to break the curse!

Oh, ya, I'm sure you're curious about what happened to Skeeter and Tick Creedy. The Creedy brothers turned their lives around after their ghostly prank experience scared the stink off of them. They turned into model citizens. In fact, my Great-Grandpa Willie employs them as the museum's tour guides. Believe it or not, they are the most requested guides in the museum! Everyone loves to hear about their real-life prank encounter with Carl's ghost... Shhhh, please don't tell them it was Jack and me, OK?

Life at home is amazing. Having Great-Grandpa Willie and Grandpa Cliff living in the mansion with my parents and me is pretty special. You should see us boys when we all get together. Laughter fills the entire mansion as our playful natures take over. Pranks are a daily part of life. I love it. My mom... not so much...

Jack is in Alaska. As agreed upon, we have been passing the Phantom Buck mount back and forth between us. He currently has the mount of The Phantom of Eerie Hollow proudly hung in his living room. He tells me that sometimes in the night, he sees the white eyes watching him....

About the Author

Clint missed a Phantom Buck a few years ago and has been haunted ever since by the memories of failure. His children believe the only way to bring their father back from such grief is to attempt to call the Phantom Buck from their Rifle Tower each hunting season. To this day, the Phantom Buck has chosen to break Clint's heart by ignoring their calls. He has truly been ghosted....